BLOODLINES

HORROR'S PAST, PRESENT, & FUTURE

I0564187

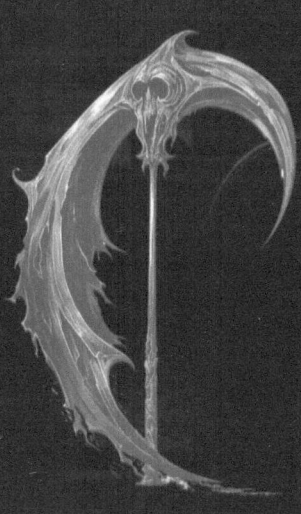

BLOODLINES

HORROR'S PAST, PRESENT, & FUTURE

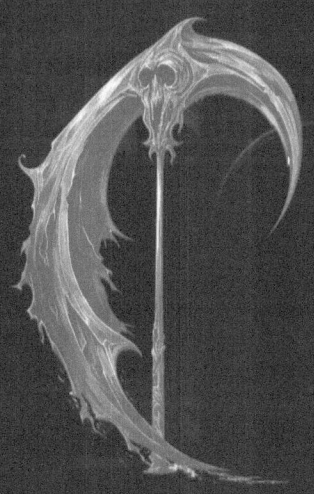

CURATED BY
KEVIN LUCIA

Welcome to the first volume of Bloodlines. I'll keep this really short, so you can dispense with my rambles quickly enough, and get to the good stuff. That's why you're here, I assume — certainly not to read a pithy and self-important sounding introduction from the likes of me.

The goal of Bloodlines is dreadfully simple. It's my humble attempt to feature the "bloodline" of the horror/speculative fiction genre. To bring together, in one place, classic stories, stories by veterans of the genre, stories by those perhaps forgotten or overlooked, stories by contemporaries, and stories written by those who represent the genre's future. That's it. That's all.

I can't claim to be an expert. I'm not an historian, nor do I have my finger on the "pulse" of the genre. I have no credibility, really, past that I love reading with every fiber of my being.

And that, my dear readers, will be my guiding light throughout this series. Me, saying to all of you: "Here are some really great stories I really love, and I hope you'll find something to appreciate in them, also."

So.

Without further ado…

Kevin Lucia
Castle Creek, NY

The Invention of Ghosts

There was no body,
Merely a book that learned how to conjure ghosts.

THE INVENTION OF GHOSTS

BY GWENDOLYN KISTE

One thing (among many things) Gwendolyn Kiste excels at is examining relationships and self-identity through the eyes of speculative fiction, fantasy, and horror. Whether its between best friends, lovers, or obsessive people in weirdly symbiotic relationships, Kiste uses horror fiction to paint terrifyingly beautiful portraits of how tortured and messy things can get between human beings, even those who love each other...so much, it often hurts.

I initially read The Invention of Ghosts in two days, when it first came out. The story left me breathless, watching the relationship between Everly and Dahlia blossom and then inevitably dissolve, as one of them disappears, and another *loses their identity to expectations and obligations. It's a powerful story I hope lingers long after you read it.*

The rapping in the ceiling came to us in September.

It was Saturday night, and we were spinning hand-me-down records in our dorm room. Iggy Pop and Siouxsie Sioux and Donovan's "Season of the Witch," even though we both agreed that last one was a bit too on-the-nose.

"What kind of witch do you want to be, Everly?" you asked me, giggling.

"Whatever witch has the most power," I said, and tried to twitch my nose.

We danced around the room together, all flailing arms and missteps, our weekend ritual of too-loud music and cold pizza left out to congeal in cardboard.

By then, we'd already been friends for years—I was sure of that much, though it was the only thing I knew. I couldn't remember the day we met. We must have been kids together once, you and me, strange and bullied and promising ourselves we'd get out of that small-town hell. But when I closed my eyes, I didn't remember any of that. All I saw were shadows where memories should be.

Out in the hall, bodies moved back and forth, a holler here, a catcall there, nearly drowning out our songs. Every weekend, the other students went free-range, wandering and carousing through the dorm, their sweat smelling like whiskey and hormones.

A figure lingered right outside, wavering there like it was eager to come in. We held our breath. In the evening, we never opened our door, not even if someone knocked. You and I were only safe together, away from the world.

"It's locked, right?" you whispered, and I nodded. With a scowl, you shoved a chair under the doorknob, just to be sure. "I wish everyone would leave us alone."

"Not everyone." I sprawled out on the floor, half-dizzy from dancing. "I wouldn't mind sharing our room with a ghost or two."

You switched out the record—*Superstition* for *Lust for Life*—and dropped the needle in the groove. "And what about people who aren't like you? What if someone doesn't want a ghost to stick around?"

I laughed. "I guess that's what exorcists are for."

You didn't usually ask me about spirits, even though they were my favorite topic. I was a history major, with a focus on the unknown. All those Victorian mystics and mesmerists and spiritualists who conjured Houdini in parlors. Uri Gellar with his spoons, and Mother Shipton with her visions—I wanted it all. I wanted their secrets. You weren't so sure yourself.

"The way you keep diving into the dark," you'd say "someday, you might get lost there."

I'd just shrug. "There are worse places to go."

You didn't know yet who you were going to be, the word *Undecided* printed in bold, accusing letters at the top of your class schedule.

"Don't worry," I would tell you at night when you couldn't sleep. "You'll figure it out."

You'd turn to me, your eyes flashing in the dark. "Promise?"

"I promise."

The speakers crackled, and still slouched on the floor, I spread out a row of vintage postcards I'd bought off eBay. Victorian figures posed in fancy parlors, their faces twisted, pale ectoplasm blossoming from their mouths. Long strings of it, stretching up into the air.

You sat cross-legged next to me. "Are any of these real?"

I shook my head. "It was all just a hoax they used back in the 1800s to sell postcards."

Yet even in the frauds, there was something to learn. Why people did it, and why others believed.

You put your hand over your own mouth, as if that might stifle ectoplasm from growing there. "What's it made of?"

"All different things," I said, gnawing my bottom lip. "Heavy cream in cheesecloth. Chewed-up paper. Whatever they could find that looked the eeriest."

We huddled together, the contorted faces in the pictures staring back at us. I moved closer, and something in the images shimmered. Just for a moment, just long enough for me to reach out, ready to awaken them, ready to draw out their magic. But you got to them first.

One by one, right down the line, you turned over all the postcards. "No more tonight," you said, shivering.

I'd upset you. I was always upsetting you.

"I'm sorry." My stomach stitched into knots. "It wasn't supposed to scare you."

You waved me off with one hand. "I'm fine," you said, and crossed to the dresser.

As you changed into your flannel pajamas, your back to me, I quietly flipped over the last picture. The face there was sullen and still. No movement, nothing at all.

The record ended, the turntable emitting blank static, and we climbed into our beds without speaking again. You were out in a minute, but I couldn't sleep, couldn't stop thinking about those pictures. Something was wrong with them, or maybe something was wrong with me. That would explain it, why my entire life had escaped me. I'd misplaced who I was, easy as forgetting where I put my house keys.

Across the room, you murmured in your sleep, and I wanted to ask you about it, about everything. Who we were, where we'd been. But it found me first. A single rapping right above us. Bodies still pushed back and forth in the hallway outside our door, but it couldn't be another party overhead. You and I lived on the top floor.

Another knock in the ceiling, and you bolted awake in your bed.

"What was that?" Your face pale as the moon. "Is something here with us?"

The room went silent again, but your fear was already rising all around us, suffocating the air from our lungs, and I curled my body tighter in my bed, just desperate to keep you calm.

"I'm sure it's nothing," I said, and closed my eyes.

BUT I COULDN'T STOP THINKING ABOUT THE RAPPING. PROBABLY just a rat, I told myself, building a nest in the plaster. That made sense. It was also wrong, and I knew it. Plus, there were the postcards. Three or four times a day, I took out the stack from under my mattress, where I'd hidden the images away so they wouldn't bother you. But no matter how long I looked at them, the faces never moved again.

Maybe I'd imagined all this. Maybe I'd envisioned ghosts where there were only shadows. I needed to find out for sure.

You came home early from class and discovered me at my desk. I never heard the door open. Instead, there you were, suddenly looming over me, staring down at a black-and-white photograph of the Fox sisters.

"The founders of the spiritualist movement," I said, even though you didn't ask. "They claimed they could communicate with ghosts."

You touched their faces, one by one. "What happened to them?"

"Nothing good." My fingers curled against the edge of the book. "They did their performances all over. Found success, even got married. Then it all fell apart."

"Why?" you asked, your voice faraway, as if you were speaking from a dream.

"Because they turned on each other."

Your gaze flicked up at me. "But they were sisters."

"It didn't matter," I said, and turned to the next page.

"Take a photograph with me," I said one morning just before Halloween.

"What will we wear?" you asked, brightening, and I smiled.

I'd enrolled in a photography class to learn about tintypes, the closest thing I could get to the old-time spirit photography. The theater department let me borrow two Victorian mourning dresses for the afternoon, and in the basement of our dorm, I'd set up a background with a red velvet curtain and two stools draped in lace.

All for our own memento mori.

"Are we supposed to be like them?" you asked when I showed you the pictures in my book, the ones with families flanking well-dressed relatives in caskets. "Are we supposed to be dead?"

"Only if you want us to be." I laughed, and you laughed too, though something in you shifted. Your mouth a rigid line, you stared off at the wall, scratching at your heavy lace collar. Ever since the rapping in the ceiling, you couldn't sleep. Sometimes, I woke up at night, and there you'd be in the next bed, your eyes colorless and distant, peering into the darkness above us. I'd always ask you what was wrong, but you never answered.

I inhaled the basement mildew, regret seeping into me. "If you'd rather not do the picture—"

"It's fine," you said, and took a seat on the temporary set.

I should have argued with you, I should have called the whole thing off, but you glanced at me again and smiled.

"Are we doing this or what?"

I set up the camera on a timer and joined you, both of us silent and waiting until the flash went off.

There was another reason I wanted the portrait. At the start of the semester, I'd gone through all my dresser drawers and the desk and even my phone. There were no pictures anywhere. Not of me or you or anyone else. My past wiped clean.

But maybe it was a good thing. People talked about second chances, clean slates. Now I had mine, an opportunity to rebuild a life, one image at a time.

In the darkroom that night, the photo came back different than I expected. Convinced I'd rigged the timer wrong, I'd moved toward the camera at the last moment, and my figure blurred out, a smear of shadows where my eyes and mouth should be. And there you were next to me, unmoving, your face wan, everything about you in startlingly sharp focus.

Sometimes, though, if I stared at us long enough, we would switch—I'd become the one in focus, and you would blur out.

I never showed you the picture. Instead, I shoved it to the back of my desk drawer and put thick folders and books on top of it. Anything to hide it away.

Anything to keep you from being afraid.

It was the end of November when I couldn't stanch your fear any longer. We were in the crowded cafeteria together at a corner table, our trays set in front of us, though neither of us was hungry.

The rapping had returned two weeks before, and while I held fast to the rat theory, you weren't convinced.

"What if it's something else?" you kept asking every night in the dark.

"It'll be okay," I promised you.

Now you sat with me, not speaking, not even when I asked you what was wrong.

"Please talk to me," I said, but my voice was gobbled up in the din of impatient students waiting in line for lunch. Someone hollered nearby and backed against our table, nearly knocking my tray to the ground. There were people everywhere, faces I didn't recognize. This whole place felt unfamiliar. Even when I glanced at you, you looked like a stranger too.

I gripped my spoon tighter, desperate to finish the rest of my coleslaw and get back to the room. Back to safety. My hands quivered, the skin burning to the bone, so hot I couldn't bear it. Everything in me burned bright, and I wanted to scream out.

Then it was over in an instant. The metal utensil turned liquid between my fingers and curled up like a fortune telling fish. I made no sound when it happened. I didn't even breathe. I just hunched over a little and stared at it, a perfect silver spiral in the palm of my hand.

A bent spoon.

This was my fault, something I'd done wrong. Something I'd conjured into being.

My heart clutched tight, I turned to you, but you pretended not to see it, even though you knew, even though your eyes darkened across the table, and you wouldn't look at me the rest of the day. I wanted to tell you it was nothing, only a silly trick I'd probably never be able to do again. No reason to blame me. After all, I was still your best friend.

If I was still your best friend.

"Be careful," you said that night before you turned out the lights, and I didn't know if it was a warning for me or for you.

WE DIDN'T TALK ABOUT WHAT HAPPENED IN THE CAFETERIA. You seemed happier that way.

"I don't want anything to come between us," you said, so I never told you about how I fell asleep in English Composition on a Monday morning, and by the time I woke up, my desk had levitated half a foot off the floor.

"She's the one," I heard the others whisper in the hallway, but when you asked what they meant, I just shrugged and pretended not to understand.

The semester ended, and with it came that long, strange stretch between fall and spring when everyone fled home for Christmas. Suitcases stuffed with dirty laundry lined the hallway, and the other students chortled and chattered and hugged goodbye, their bus stubs or plane tickets in hand.

You and I were from the same town—if I focused hard enough, I could almost imagine the outline of your house— but you didn't want to go back there.

"Stay here with me," you said, and because I didn't want to leave you alone, I agreed.

Overnight, the campus became a haunted, empty place. No classes, no open cafeteria, just the two of us marooned together, with a quart of Aristocrat Vodka and a dozen packages of peanut butter sandwich crackers we'd emptied out of the vending machine.

When we'd eaten everything in the dorm our quarters could buy us, we walked down the block in the subzero weather to the 7/11, our arms looped together, and with our last two dollars, we picked out two cans of Campbell's chicken noodle soup.

Back in our room with no microwave, we giggled and ate the soup cold, slurping every drop out with plastic sporks.

"I wish it could always be this way," you said.

I smiled. "So do I."

This was okay. We were all right again, you and me. No more fear crackling behind your eyes, no glancing away from me because of what you'd seen, what I'd done.

After our makeshift dinner, you tethered the empty soup cans together with your bootlaces and strung them between our beds.

"My own homespun magic," you said with a grin.

All night, we colluded in the dark, our secrets passed back and forth along that single taut string. There was a world in those shadows that no one else could ever touch.

"Did we do this when we were kids?" I whispered.

"Don't you remember?" you asked, your voice warbling inside the ribbed metal, as though you were a thousand miles away.

I didn't answer. Instead, I turned over in bed, still clutching the tin can, as your distant whispers lulled me to sleep.

"TEACH ME SOMETHING," YOU SAID. "A TRICK YOU'VE LEARNED from those books."

It was a snowstorm in February, and the first time we'd talked about this in months.

I brought out the Ouija board, the one I'd packed in my luggage. It must have come from our life before this, from some quaint little department store in our hometown I wished I could remember.

You turned off the overhead light, and I lit a chime candle, the wax deep red and stippled with herbs. This was it, my chance to prove to you there was nothing to fear. The planchette quivered beneath our fingers in the dark, the air glinting around us. For a moment, I could hear everything. A creak deep in the plaster of the walls. The gentle thrum of our heartbeats in tandem.

Something was coming through, blinking in and out, like camera flashes. An image, our faces maybe. There were other things too. Salt between my fingers, and the smell of citrus, sweet and heady. This belonged to us, a memory rising up out of the earth, out of an icy past that reached toward me.

I leaned forward, ready to seize it before it escaped, but you cried out suddenly and wrenched your hand away, the connection instantly lost.

"I can't," you said, your voice splitting in two. "I can't do this."

Panic tightened in my throat. "It's okay, don't worry about it."

I reached out for you, but you moved away from me, all the way to the other side of the room. An aching quiet settled around us, as heavy as regret, the silence punctuated only by the rise and fall of whiskey-soaked voices in the room next to ours.

"Maybe you could teach me something now," I said at last. "About us. About where we're from. How did we meet?"

You stared back at me, your eyes gone dim and vacant. "Don't you remember anything? Don't you remember *me*?"

"Of course, I do," I said, almost breathless, but it wasn't true. I wouldn't have asked you otherwise.

After that, I pretended I was someone else with you. A girl who would never fraternize with spirits or bend metal or levitate by accident. I wouldn't let you see me reading my books on Mother Shipton, and if I heard the rapping in the ceiling, I would just close my eyes and wish it away.

If only everyone else could forget too. After the desk incident in the fall, the other kids wanted to know how I did it.

"This is the chick I told you about." That was how a guy from my photography class introduced me to his friends. You and I were in his dorm room, though neither of us liked it there. The place was smaller than ours, and it reeked of sweat and stale Doritos.

We'd only stopped by for a minute, for me to drop off some class notes in exchange for a book on spirit photography the guy claimed to own. There was no book. This was a trap. They'd gotten me here, so I could be the evening's entertainment. I wanted to run, but you'd already slipped away to the corner, leaving me to talk to people I'd never met in a room I was desperate to escape.

"So you know magic," said a boy whose name was Ralph or Ron or Robbie. He smiled at me, and for a moment, I almost wasn't scared.

Next to him, a girl with violet eyeliner grunted and took a swig of cheap beer. "Like how to pull a rabbit out of a hat?"

I shrugged. "Something like that."

All night, they passed around cheap fifths of booze, as I made ashtrays and shot glasses and beer bottles float. For hours, we played *Light as a feather, stiff as a board*, everybody getting their turn at flying. Everybody except you.

You sat alone on the floor, not playing our games, pretending you didn't even notice us, everything about you becoming smaller and stranger. My chest tightened, and I missed you. I missed my best friend, even though you were sitting right there.

"Do you want to leave?" I mouthed from across the room, but you just stared off, your eyes unfocused, never seeing me.

A beer bottle floated past, but I kept looking at you, right at you. Only you weren't there anymore, not completely. I could see straight through you, your body translucent as water.

With my breath stifled in my chest, I blinked, and you returned.

The bottles cascaded to the floor, and everyone in the room called for an encore.

"No more tonight," I said, my gaze still on you, part of me convinced if I turned away, you'd vanish for good.

The others groaned. "But things were just getting interesting," they said, and hands reached out for me from all directions, grasping and groping as I backed away.

"Leave her alone," Ralph or Robbie said, but it didn't stop the rest of them. The guy from my photography class tried to block my way, but I managed to grab your arm and pull you toward the door.

"What happened to you?" I asked back in our room.

"I'm fine," you said without inflection. "Everything's fine."

But that wasn't true, and we both knew it. The next day, the turntable sat in silence all afternoon, neither of us stirring from our beds, not even to order takeout. We needed to talk. We needed to do something, even if we couldn't figure out what that was.

"You like it too much," you said that evening, sprawled across your mattress, sheets in a tangle around you. "And you show off with it. It's dangerous."

Moonlight leaked in between the slats of the venetian blinds, casting shadows across you, making your body look like you were sliced into pieces.

"Why are the things I want so terrible to you?" I asked.

You stared at me, your gaze defiant. "Why are they so important to you? Why can't you just be happy with the way things are?"

My stomach twisted. I couldn't tell you how I wanted these secrets, because then maybe I'd remember what came before.

Maybe I'd remember me.

A knock at the door, and everything in the world held still. You and I looked at each other, not moving, as voices seeped in from the hallway. The kids from last night's party, looking for another round of magic.

They knocked again, and with a sigh, I got up from my bed. "I'll tell them to go."

"Don't unlock it," you whispered, but it was already too late. The door swung open, and they poured inside, the ones from the party, along with their friends, and their friends of friends, all pushing to get a front row seat.

"Everybody's eager to meet you, honey," the girl with violet eyeliner said, and our room never felt so huge and so small at the same time.

I backed against the wall, feeling like an invader in my own life. I wanted to send them away. I wanted to lock the door and hide here with you. But I already knew no one was leaving until they saw what I could do.

Creeping backward into the room, I reached out for you, and you grasped for my hand, but there were too many of them, the wave of their restless bodies shoving between us and carrying you away from me.

More of them clambered in, and I couldn't see you anymore. You'd abandoned me here to contend with them and their demands to see me perform.

So perform I did. With everyone gathered around the Ouija board, a spirit told us her name was Rhee, and she warned me about the water. Whatever that meant.

The next morning, after everyone had gone, you were back, sitting on your bed as though you'd never left.

"Why?" was all you'd say.

For a week, you wouldn't leave the room, not for class or the cafeteria or even the shower.

I kneeled at your bedside. "What can I do?" I asked, but you wouldn't answer.

You still didn't know who you wanted to be. But you sure knew what you didn't want—to turn out like me.

Finally, with the silence too heavy to bear, I had to try something, anything else. I put one of the tin cans on your bed, and I strung the other to my side of the room.

"I'm sorry," I whispered into it.

"No, you're not." Your voice trilled through the metal, but I was looking right at you there on the bed. Your gaze set on the ceiling, you weren't moving, you weren't speaking, yet I could hear you all the same.

"But I *am* sorry," I said. "It won't happen again. No more séances."

You turned to me, your eyes flickering the color of ash. "Promise?"

"I promise," I said, swallowing down the words that stuck in my throat like glue, and I already knew you didn't believe me.

A WEEK BEFORE FINALS, YOU STOLE ALL MY BOOKS. *THE MAGUS*, and *The Book of Thoth*, and the biographies about the Fox Sisters and Madame Blavatsky and Mother Shipton, each tome hidden away under privet shrubs in the quad or behind a row of washers in the basement of the dorm.

I stood in front of you in our room, gripping a soggy copy of *Thought-Forms* that I'd rescued from the dumpster next to the theater building. "Please don't do this."

You shrugged. "I'm not doing anything," you said, so nonchalant about it that I almost believed you.

I had to take my exams from memory. Somehow, every grade came back an A.

"See?" you said afterward. "You didn't need to study anyway."

That night, I went walking among shadows and forgotten spirits. All campuses were strange, spectral places, even if the brochures never bragged about it. Too many broken dreams not to be haunted.

The rain came, a heavy spring storm, but I didn't go back to you, not right away.

When I got home after midnight, shivering and soaked to the marrow, you brought me a towel and wrapped it around me.

"Forgive me?" you whispered like a frightened child, and because I couldn't think of anything else, I just nodded.

I WAS ALREADY PACKED FOR SUMMER BREAK WHEN YOU TOLD ME about the internship.

"It's perfect for us," you said, your smile brighter than I'd ever seen it. "It's right here on campus. We don't even have to swap rooms."

You'd already filled out applications in my name and yours, and we'd both been accepted. This was your way of making it all up to me, a way to prove we were still best friends.

But I shook my head. "I'd rather go home," I said. "I haven't been back in over a year."

Though for all I could remember, I hadn't been there at all. I wanted to see it again. I wanted to meet my parents, maybe meet yours too.

"Why go back to that place?" You exhaled a sharp laugh. "We did everything we could to get out of there."

"Because," I said, and a quiet rage bubbled up in me, so potent that my lips couldn't form the words to finish the sentence.

You sensed this in me, the finality of it, and something in your face softened. "We'll visit at the end of the summer," you said. "The last two weeks of August. I promise."

I shouldn't have said yes. I shouldn't have done a lot of things.

The internship was all filing, the kind of grunt work they just didn't want to pay someone for, but you didn't seem to mind.

"Don't you love how quiet the campus is?" you'd ask on Saturday nights, the hallway outside dark and abandoned, and I'd always smile. Maybe this was what we needed, the two of us shipwrecked away from the world. I told myself that things would be different. We'd start the next semester, and you'd choose a major, and then we'd dance again in the dorm and eat cold soup out of the can and laugh until we forgot what was funny.

It wouldn't always be so hard.

At the end of July, our class schedules arrived, and I gaped at the calendar. The semester started earlier this year. August 15th, the day after our internship ended.

"There's no time for us to go home now," I said.

You shrugged. "Maybe for Thanksgiving?"

But we wouldn't go home together then either. I was afraid we'd never go home again.

That evening, when you were down the hall in the shower, I thumbed through your phone. Not a single picture of us from back home. I had no proof of me from before. It was as if I didn't exist at all.

BY THE TIME THE SEMESTER STARTED, I COULDN'T CONTROL IT anymore. In class, I had to bungee my desk legs to the radiator if I didn't want to float to the ceiling. Every spoon I touched curled up in my grasp, so many that I could barely finish a meal. I tucked the mangled silverware under my pillow, beneath my bed, behind the bookshelf. Anything to keep you from finding them.

Each day, the lunch woman scowled at me when I shuffled through the cafeteria line. She knew it was me squirreling away all the spoons, even if she couldn't prove it, even if she didn't know why.

"It's theft," she whispered, as she heaved a helping of congealed meatloaf on my tray. "I could get you expelled for it."

I nodded and thanked her for the slop. Part of me wished I could tell her about it, confess to someone about the shame I had stashed away in the dark places of my room. But she wouldn't understand. Nobody would.

Between classes, I sneaked down to the 7/11 and filled my pockets with plastic spoons. It was safer for everyone that way.

On Friday nights, I went to parties without you. I gazed into bowls of dark ink to divine a future I couldn't see, and I made whole beds float off the floor and crash into ceilings, chunks of plaster crumbling to the carpet like snow, but I kept my promise to you. No séances, even though I couldn't see what difference it made, especially since you weren't even there. You barely left our room now.

"You can come too," I told you, but you waved me off with one hand.

"Have fun," you said, not looking at me, never looking at me.

So I went out and did my best impression of a person. It was almost a passable performance. At least the other kids acknowledged me when I did tricks for them.

The boy from the first party—Robbie was definitely his name, I asked him three times—even invited me out to see a Kubrick film at the arthouse theater across town. He paid for my ticket and bought me popcorn. Afterward, we kissed in the backseat of his used Subaru, a sea of greasy Butterfinger and Lays potato chip wrappers crackling beneath us, and I liked it, only because it helped me pretend I was a normal girl. Someone who went out to movies and made out in cars.

Someone who knew where she'd been and where she might be going.

All night, whenever he wasn't kissing me, he talked about his family and the score for the football game and sports movies I'd never seen. He was the kind of boy who was sweet enough but so terribly clueless. A guy like him couldn't fathom a place with girls like you and me in it, so he just lived in another world that looked like ours but wasn't, somewhere that was clean and safe and kind.

I envied him for that delusion. I hated him for it too.

I got back to our room after midnight, and you were already asleep. I thought about waking you and telling you about my date. Then we could have laughed about the candy bar wrappers and the silly sports films and the ridiculousness of it all.

I lingered there in the dark, trying to decide what to do.

Then a single rapping echoed in the ceiling, and I crawled into bed without a word, my face buried in the curves of my pillow, muffling a scream you couldn't hear anyhow.

YOU WERE STUDYING LATE IN THE LIBRARY WHEN I LIT THE candles in a circle.

This was against the rules you'd set for me, but I had to remember. I deserved to remember.

There was a party down the hall, and you'd forgotten to lock the door on your way out. A quick knock, and the guy from my photography class came inside without being invited. The planchette already in my hand, I stared up at him from the floor. He smirked at me before shooting a look over his shoulder.

"Séance!" he yelled, and then they were everywhere. Robbie and all the others from before, shoving to get a closer look at the Ouija board.

The girl with violet eyeliner shot me an ugly grin from the doorway. "Who are you talking to this time, Everly?"

"Myself," I said.

Someone passed around a bottle of Dekuyper peach schnapps, and I chugged half of it, trying to steady myself for what came next.

The drip candles burned down, the wicks smoldering, and I closed my eyes.

"Show me," I whispered to the dark. "Show me *anything*."

It came in smoke and fragments, a mosaic of us. You and me, somewhere far off, the smell of citrus almost suffocating. We were younger then, but not children. Almost grown. Almost us.

"Someday," you said. "We'll forget them."

"Forget who?" I asked, both in my voice and the voice of the me I'd lost.

But I didn't get my answer. All at once, I jolted back into myself, into the present. The door had swung open, and jaundice-yellow light flooded the room.

"You promised."

You were standing on the other side, the hallway so bright that your figure was nothing but shadow.

I understood it now, understood it too late. You didn't want me to remember.

"How could you do this?" you asked, your words distorted like an echo. Like you were already lost to me.

"I'm sorry," I said, but my voice was eaten alive in the ruckus of college students, calling out for more, always more.

My chest constricted, and I reached for you, but you were too far away, and I was far too late.

Your body dissolved to gray, everything in you fading out, as though the air itself was swallowing you whole. Then, with a final sob, you were gone.

"Nice trick," the girl with violet eyeliner said, and I retched up peach schnapps all over the carpet.

I STILL COULDN'T REMEMBER THE DAY WE MET. IT WAS A MEMORY that should never have left me. I should have held onto it, cherished it like a prized heirloom, tucked it away for safekeeping.

After all, when a person made a mistake like this, they ought to remember what got them there.

There was no body to recover, no inquest on your behalf.

"She went of her own free will," everyone concluded, as though you were merely an ordinary runaway, and that was that.

Only you weren't really gone. None of my books ever told me this, maybe because nobody knew except me—that a person didn't have to die to become a ghost. You just needed to want it badly enough.

After you vanished, no one came to pick up your things. No parents or siblings or other next of kin. That meant I inherited everything of yours—your clothes and your turntable and your tin can telephone.

All night, I played your favorite records. "Season of the Witch" and "Peek-a-Boo" and "Lust for Life," anything that might coax you back.

"Can you hear it?" I asked the ceiling, and turned it up a little louder just to be sure.

Soon, this was all I did, sealed up in our room like a tomb, desperate to bring you back from beyond. I stopped bothering to head down to the cafeteria where the lunch lady still glared at me, or the showers where the other girls always inched a couple steps away, quietly terrified they might meet the same fate as you if they got too close. Robbie brought me pizza, but sometimes, I wouldn't even open the door when he knocked. Why bother? It hadn't gotten you and me very far the last time I unlocked that door and let in the world.

I stopped going to class too. It seemed pointless now. Besides, college had already taught us everything we needed to know. I learned how to conjure ghosts, and you learned how to be one.

"Where are you?" I whispered over and over, but not even the walls creaked back.

THEY KICKED ME OUT A SEMESTER BEFORE GRADUATION.

"We're sorry about what happened to your roommate," the assistant dean said, his owl eyes peering at me across a cluttered desk. "But we all agree perhaps a leave of absence would be in the best interest of all involved."

As in, the interest of everyone who'd reported a strange smell coming from my room and had thought that I'd actually died in there. It was just the pile of rotting pepperoni pizzas stacked waist-high in the corner.

"We'll figure it out," Robbie said when I told him goodbye. He sounded sincere about it too, as though the girl he'd barely dated was his responsibility or something.

"It's for the best," I said, and almost believed it. I figured I should leave you alone in your self-imposed afterlife. That only seemed fair.

My mistake, however, was believing you wanted claim over the campus. It turned out you only wanted claim over me. On the bus ride out of town, you took up the seat next to mine. I couldn't see you there, but when I closed my eyes, I could hear both our heartbeats.

For the first time, I went home. I hoped it would stir some memory, wrench me back into myself, but when the "Welcome to" sign crested over the highway, my resolve crumbled to dust.

The buildings smeared past the bus windows, as unfamiliar as an undiscovered country. It was just another town, another speck on a nothing map.

My parents picked me up at the station and took me on a tour of our house, like I was a first-time visitor.

"It's nice," I said, and meant it.

I never mentioned you to them. I never asked if they remembered you or if they could sense you here with me, that pulse that never stopped thrumming beneath your invisible skin.

My mother fixed meatloaf and twice-baked potatoes for supper, and we ate as a family at the dinner table, surrounded with generic paintings of bucolic settings I'd never seen. All the while, my lips desperate to form the words for the things I wanted to know.

Why didn't you call me at college? Why weren't you worried when I never came home to visit?

But I didn't ask, and they never told.

At night, I wandered the downtown streets alone, past the ancient clocktower that was always five minutes behind, tallying up the landmarks. That city park over there where we must have played, up and down on the seesaw, and the community pool, where we probably learned to swim, with orange floaties on our arms. I waited for it to all come back to me, but every memory remained stubbornly out of reach.

After he picked up a diploma I'd never see, Robbie came to visit me, and after only a few more dates, he asked me to marry him, right there in front of my parents at Sunday supper.

"Why?" I blurted out.

"Because I love you," he said, and I nearly laughed in his face over that one. Robbie was a timeline guy, his life a sequential checklist of expectations. He'd already graduated, and now he'd get married. It just so happened I was the lucky girl around at exactly the right time.

Though I barely knew him, I had no reason to say no. He was so grounded, so achingly normal. This was what I should do, as though tethering myself to a steady ship might save me from you.

The next week, he and I moved in together, everything a whirlwind of U-Haul boxes and a flash of light off a diamond that never quite fit my finger.

"What are these?" he asked when he found my cache of curled spoons, stuffed in the bottom of a ratty backpack.

I shrugged. "Just an old parlor trick of mine."

"What a waste of perfectly good silverware," he said and tossed them in the trash.

A thorn twisted in my chest, but I just smiled and kept unpacking.

I waited until he went to work. When I was sure he wouldn't double-back, I put my arm elbow-deep in coffee grinds and used Kleenex to retrieve them. There was no reason I needed the spoons, no reason except they were mine, these tarnished souvenirs of who I almost was. A girl with arcane aspirations, secrets she planned to unravel.

But when I finally pulled them out of the garbage, my breath caught, and I gagged up a sob.

All the handles had been straightened. You'd gotten there first.

"How about a spring wedding?" Robbie asked. "Or a date in the fall? Winter ceremonies are nice too."

This was how we spent every weekend: speculating about the future I wasn't sure I had.

"Maybe spring," I'd say, but April and May came and went, and we sent no invitations.

"Next June then," he said, but on July Fourth, I was still no Missus. I kept pushing back the inevitable, hoping to drive you away first. He and I couldn't start a new life together, not with you looming over the honeymoon suite.

The third year of our engagement, and Robbie's ears turned red.

"I won't wait anymore," he said, and finally, all my choices had evaporated.

"September," I agreed, and he smiled and kissed me hard on the mouth and embossed it on ivory, just to make it official.

There were so many things he wanted. A horse-drawn carriage to take us from a church that neither of us attended. A cake stacked so high it looked like a Jenga game ready to topple. And engagement photos, those cheesy pictures staged in some comically rustic setting.

Robbie and I posed together for two hours and two hundred dollars, grinning at each other on a tractor we couldn't drive and in a barn we didn't own. I listened for you, but you weren't there with us. No dual heartbeat, no whispers, no rapping in the rotted wood.

Maybe I could put you behind me after all. Maybe I didn't need a past to have a future. I'd settle in and build a decent life, a normal life. This would be okay.

A few days later, the photographer called our apartment.

"There's a problem," he said on the other end, and I went alone to his studio.

"It doesn't make sense," he said, and handed me the prints. "Double exposures like that should only happen on film."

I flipped through the photographs, one by one, my heart seizing in my chest each time.

All the pictures had turned out the same—with your face superimposed over mine, the two of us blurred together, our eyes and mouths no more than a smear of shadow.

I paid the photographer in cash to hand over the prints and delete the files. Then I burned all the pictures on the Weber grill in my parents' backyard, the plastic facsimiles of our faces bubbling and melting between the grates.

"What are you doing?" My mother charged out of the house, her hands cupped over her face to ward off the smoke, but I said nothing. I just watched to make sure every trace of you burned.

You hadn't left me. You'd never leave.

At home, I dug your tin cans out of a box I'd hidden under the bed when I moved in. My throat dry, I held the metal opening up to my ear.

"You're not sorry," you whispered, your voice as crisp as autumn. "You'll never be sorry."

Everything in me went weak. Here you were after all these years. I could hear you any time of day.

I should have tossed the cans in the trash. I should have buried them deeper than a grave.

Instead on the morning of my wedding, already zipped up into my white satin dress, I pulled them out of the box again.

"Will you be happy?" You chortled at me. "Will we ever be happy?"

"Time to go, darling," my mother called from the other room, and I dropped the tin cans at the sound of her voice. But it didn't matter. You just kept chattering there on the carpet, never resting, never waning, murmuring all the lies I feared were the truth.

I inched toward the doorway. "Be right there, Mom," I said, a sob lodged in my throat.

At the back door of the church, my mother dropped me off, so I wouldn't have to walk more than a few steps in my pristine silk heels.

"Meet you inside," she said, beaming, and I waited until she drove around to the front of the parking lot, before I slipped off my shoes and took off barefoot in the grass and gravel.

A runaway bride that couldn't run fast enough. Not if I wanted to escape you.

For hours, I hid beneath the clocktower, ducking behind rusted metal, my hem unraveling in the briars and weeds, as they called out for me.

"Everly, where are you?" Robbie hollered, his voice splintering.

"Darling, please come back." My mother, so desperate I almost gave in.

Somewhere close, my father grunted. "Don't make a fool of yourself, girl."

I curled in the dirt, my veil ripped in two, the bottoms of my feet bleeding. I never should have accepted his proposal. My life wasn't a timetable like Robbie's. Marrying him wouldn't have fixed anything. Instead, it would have made everything so much worse. For him. For me. Even for you.

Eventually, when night came and all hope of a proper reconciliation had been abandoned, they gave up. I wondered where they went afterward or if someone at least got to enjoy that skyscraper-high cake.

I TRIED TO BURY YOUR GHOST IN THE EARTH, INTERRING YOUR remains so deep and rotting that even the worms wouldn't touch what was left.

Your records and flannel pajamas and the tintype picture of us, all deposited in the dirt past the county line. The tin can telephone went too, and as I dropped it into the chasm at my feet, your voice echoed from inside the metal.

"You promised, Everly."

My eyes blurred with tears. "I'm sorry," I said, and shoveled heavy earth over you, hoping with everything in me that you would stay there.

I did my best to shape a life of my own. I got an efficiency apartment in town, and I found work and lost it again and then found something else, all of it the same thing anyhow. Folders to file, spreadsheets to email, jobs that were almost as dead-end as you and me.

Soon, a month was gone, and then a year, and finally so much time had passed that I had to look at a calendar to track it. My life was vanishing around me, and only you were here to keep me company.

I told myself it didn't have to be this way. At a Sunday Brunch where the French toast was soggy around the edges, I tried to reconnect with people from college, though I almost couldn't recognize any of them. The girl with violet eyeliner didn't wear that color anymore. She had a job at the bank now, approving and denying mortgages, voting up or down on other people's dreams.

"The bosses don't like too much makeup," she said, and sipped a Bloody Mary. "And besides, I got sick of that look myself. A bit much, don't you think?"

I had barely known these people on campus. Now they were all complete strangers to me, the kind who did things in college but managed to forget all the parts that didn't benefit them. I tried to talk about you, about what happened, but even though they'd been right there that night, they hardly remembered it.

"The ghost, right?" They'd forgotten your name. If they ever knew it in the first place.

"But she's been gone for years now," said the guy who didn't do photography anymore. He munched on a greasy strip of bacon, even as you swirled around us, bits of you dripping into the clotted cream on my dessert plate.

"She's already a ghost," the girl with no eyeliner said. "Probably about time to let her rest, don't you think, Everly?"

I nodded, and wished I could.

Before I paid the check, one of the girls invited everyone to her New Year's Eve party.

"That sounds nice," I said and told her I'd attend. I shouldn't want to spend any more time with these people. But this was a chance, a break in the cycle. I could start again, be someone different. I could do better this time.

I bought a new dress and new silver heels at the mall, and I even brushed my hair for the occasion. A quick glance in the mirror, and I almost looked like me.

At the party, the hostess welcomed me with a stiff smile, and I stood along the wall, gripping a champagne glass, trying to remember everyone's names.

"Clair," I whispered to myself. "Or maybe Carla. Connie?" I'd never been very good at this.

Of course, there was one name I couldn't forget. Robbie. I hadn't seen him in four years, not since the night before our would-be wedding. He'd had another more successful trip to the altar in the meantime. She stood at his side, beaming, her belly already swelled with a bundle of good tidings. Another item ticked off the checklist. A life within a life.

Jealousy stirred within me, nearly choking off my air. Except I didn't envy her for having him. I envied her for not having you. She'd never know what it was like to be haunted, to carry a ghost in her bones. Her life had turned out in a way mine never would.

Across the room, the hostess hugged Robbie and nodded in my direction. I sipped my champagne, the truth clenching in my gut. This had all been a trap. Inviting me here was a way for Robbie to show off his new life to the girl who destroyed his old one. I should have guessed nobody would invite me anywhere without a reason.

"She used to do magic," Robbie said when someone asked about me. He grinned and pulled his new bride in closer. "Everly, show them a trick, why don't you?"

Everyone turned to watch me, their faces blank as fresh paper, waiting to see what I could conjure.

My chest tightened, and I stared into the depths of my champagne glass.

"I don't remember how anymore," I said, and realized it was true. I'd wanted so much to forget what went wrong between you and me that I forgot the good too. All those secrets I'd done my best to decipher. They were lost to me now.

Before midnight, I returned home alone, my silver heels and resolutions abandoned by the door. The bare apartment greeted me the only way it knew how—with you. I couldn't conjure my old tricks anymore, but you could.

With a rapping in the ceiling, in the walls, behind the door. My bed floating half a foot in the air. And your tin can telephone, caked with dirt and earthworms, set in the middle of the kitchen counter.

"It's fine," your voice warbled in the mud. "Everything's fine."

My knees turned liquid, and I inched away from you until my back pressed into the plaster. Then I slid to the floor and collapsed in the corner, cradling my head in my hands. There would be no fixed-up version of me, no New Year-New You. This was it—all we'd ever had, all we would ever get.

"Don't you remember, Everly?" you said, and my lips parted to exhale a scream or a sob or anything at all, but no sound came out.

I TRIED TO DROWN YOU.

With vodka in a shot glass.

With water overflowing in a bathtub.

With the heavy sound of music thrumming in my ears.

This should have worked. This should have freed me from you, my body bobbing in lukewarm bathwater, eyes gone milky and vacant, scrying into the beyond, into places where even you hadn't been.

But this world wasn't ready to let go of me just yet. Armed with sirens and stretchers, the men in white came and pulled me out of the dark and bandaged up my wrists before I could tell them not to bother.

They put me in a room not much bigger than the one in our dorm, and they left me there alone with you. The only thing I didn't want was what they gave me.

The next morning, the gauze itchy on my wrists, I met with a doctor who didn't believe in ghosts. He cared more about focusing on the childhood I couldn't remember.

"Did you have a good relationship with your mom and dad?"

I shrugged. "I guess so."

Afterward, I caught a glimpse of his notes.

At the time of the attempt, patient was playing "Season of the Witch" on repeat.

The sentence was underlined three times in accusing red pen. I couldn't help but laugh. Everyone here was as afraid of me as you always were.

"Don't worry, honey," the nurse cooed. "We'll make you strong again."

The sting of that word, the built-in accusation. *Strong.* What did they know of strength anyhow? They all had their assumptions of how they'd do things differently. But how could you fight what wasn't there, a presence thinner than mist yet heavier than heartache? Were their pills and pens and empty promises really stronger than me? Because nobody weak had ever survived so long shackled to a ghost like you.

AFTER THREE NIGHTS UNDER OBSERVATION, THEY SENT ME home. Less than seventy-two hours, and I was spit back into a world you owned.

Except nobody trusted me now. I'd lost my last job, and the landlord had warned me I was a week from eviction, and that was before the tub overflowed, and my downstairs neighbor thought to call 911. That meant for the first time I could ever remember, I became my parents' responsibility.

"You should have told us," my mother said on the ride home, her face scrunched up and red from crying.

In the backseat, my whole life sat next to me, crammed inside a single bin. My parents had emptied out my apartment, and this was everything I owned, including a keepsake of you. Through the clear plastic, your tin can telephone glinted inside. They shouldn't have brought you here too, not that it would have mattered what I told them. Even if they'd thrown you out, you'd just dig yourself out of the ends of the earth, wouldn't you?

At home, my mother ushered me upstairs. "You know which one's your room," she said, before she added, "The first door on the right."

"Thanks," I said.

Because I didn't know what else to do with you, the plastic bin went into the back of my closet. With all my strength, I pushed it as far as it would go, but it snagged on something in the corner. A small box, no bigger than a turntable. The lid slid off, and my heart held tight in my chest. Maybe we'd be inside, you and me, proof of who we once were. Maybe I'd finally meet my own face.

But it was only a stack of undeveloped Polaroids, the film as cloudy and inscrutable as thick fog.

That night, as I curled in my bed beneath faded Care Bears sheets, I listened for you in the walls. Did you know this place? How many sleepovers did we have here in this room when we were kids?

I bet my mother remembered you, her daughter's best friend growing up. I almost felt sorry for her and my dad. It must have been hard having me around. The girl who failed at college, failed at the altar, even failed at dying.

"You can move past this," she promised me, but how could she honestly believe that? You'd obliterated everything else in my life like the passing of the moon blotting out the noonday sun.

At the breakfast table each morning, they could see you swirling around me.

My mother frowned, her immaculate acrylic nails drumming on her placemat. "Have you tried asking her politely to leave?"

"Yes, Mom," I said, sighing. "I've asked her politely to go."

"Have you tried asking not-so-politely?" My father slammed down his coffee mug, shaking the whole table. "Sometimes, you've got to be forceful with these things."

He talked like a man who'd met many ghosts in his time and negotiated each one right out of his life.

"I've done that too, Dad."

My mother filled my glass to the brim with orange juice, as though all I needed to get rid of my ghost problem was enough Vitamin C to drown in. "Then we'll have to try something else," she said.

So on a Sunday afternoon, they called in an exorcist.

"He's a very nice man," my mother assured me, and put on her best cotton frock, the same one she wore to my almost-wedding. My father picked out a favorite tie and even donned the shiny dress shoes that squeaked.

"Is this an exorcism or a funeral?" I asked, and wondered if maybe it was both.

Since nobody bothered to tell me the dress code, I just wore a pair of jeans and a stained T-shirt of some band I couldn't pick out of a lineup.

The priest arrived an hour late, all stone-faced and sour, a bottle of holy water tucked under his arm like a cheap fifth of whiskey.

I sat on the couch, my legs drawn up under me. "Should you strap me down or something? Would that help?"

The priest shook his head. He wasn't as talkative as I expected. I figured he'd be all Bible verses and brimstone and "the power of Christ compels you." Instead, he barely even looked at me. Already I could guess what he was thinking: even God knew I was a lost cause.

He opened up a small notepad, and I strained to get a look at his list of exorcisms that had come before, but the page was blank.

"How did the spirit die?"

I bit off a piece of skin from my bottom lip. "She didn't," I said. "She just decided to vanish."

A long pause. "The spirit is alive?"

"I guess so," I said. "Turns out a person doesn't have to die to become a ghost. They can just really want to be one."

The priest hesitated, and I was waiting for him to argue with me or call me godless or a liar, but he just shook his head again. "I never knew that."

"Neither did I," I said.

The priest did his best, I'd give him that. I just about drowned in the holy water he dumped on my head, and for a little while, he even had me believing that if I kept the tears flowing and the blessed mantras on repeat, then maybe I could be free of you. But it didn't make any difference. You never appeared when he cast you out. You weren't there at all. We threw a soiree in your honor, and you didn't even bother to show up. I should have expected this. You always did hate parties.

After the exorcism failed, the priest pocketed his money, and my parents took me out to dinner, as though a plate of prime rib was a proper consolation prize under the circumstances.

"Don't worry, honey," my mother said, scowling at her Caesar salad. "We'll figure something out."

Except there wasn't much left to do. We were out of reasonable options and almost out of unreasonable ones too. Whatever tethered you to me was proving impossible to sever.

I AWOKE IN BED THAT NIGHT TO A RAPPING IN THE CEILING, AND my lungs clogged. Everything in the room shimmered around me, and I clutched my throat, choking up clouds of white all over the mattress. The substance kept coming, kept dripping down my chin and onto the bedsheets, the taste like curdled cream and wet paper.

Globs of ectoplasm, just like the postcards I showed you. Except unlike those vintage pictures, this haunting was no hoax. You'd gifted me the real thing.

When at last I caught my breath, I stumbled out of bed, needing water, needing to scream, but I nearly slipped on something in the dark. Spilled out on the floor was the box of undeveloped Polaroids. I kneeled next to them, examining each blank image, placing them in neat rows, one by one. Rocking back and forth, the acrid taste still in my mouth, I squinted at the film, until something seized up inside me.

These weren't undeveloped. They were erased. It was as if you were daring me to remember.

And maybe I could. Back at school, I'd done things nobody could explain. If I tried hard enough, if I conjured all the secrets left in me, perhaps I could bring these photos back again.

I picked a single image, and with my breath steady, I focused. This time, I didn't need candles or a spirit board or holy water. I just needed me.

My fingers burned, as the image bubbled and shifted. There we were, you and me in front of a pale shotgun house. *Your* house. Two streets behind the downtown clocktower.

I could find this place. I could find where you'd come from.

On foot, it took me ten minutes. Only a moment really, yet the longest walk I'd ever made.

The property wasn't quite the same as the photograph. A *For Sale* sign stood sentry in the yard, with waist-high weeds overgrown around it. A forsaken home, the yellowed paint peeling from the siding.

I wondered if anyone still lived here. How they could still live here. I knocked anyway. A rustling inside, and the porch light flicked on. I held my breath, as the door opened.

"Yeah?" A voice like gravel and metal. The voice of your mother.

She looked a little like you, only sadder. Her eyes creased at the corners, brow knit as though she'd forgotten how to smile years ago.

With a cigarette in her hand, she nodded at me. "You here to look at the house?"

I gaped back at her. It was almost one in the morning, and she honestly thought someone might want to tour the place at this time of night.

I swayed in place, shaking my head.

She shrugged. "Then what do you want?"

This wasn't going the way I'd hoped. I steadied myself against the doorframe, so close to the past now.

"Just to talk," I said.

A rueful laugh. "I'm not much of a talker, kid."

She looked ready to close the door, ready to seal me out, all your secrets still safe inside.

"I'm a friend of your daughter's," I blurted out, though it was a lie. You and I hadn't been friends for a long time.

Your mother pursed her lips at me. "I don't have a daughter."

"No," I said, "but you did."

At this, she scoffed, and I was sure it was over, that I was about to be locked out for good, but when she retreated into the house, she left the door open behind her.

I creeped inside, into the world that used to belong to you.

"So you knew my girl." Your mother settled on a couch as withered as she was. "Not many people can say that. An odd one, that child. Never could figure her out."

I huddled in the far corner, trying and failing to find something that looked familiar. "What was so strange about her?"

Your mother tilted her head, as if taken aback. "I was hoping you could tell me. Like I said, I never figured her out."

"Neither did I."

We were quiet for what felt like forever, before she motioned to my bandaged wrists. "Did she do that?"

"No," I said and tugged my sleeves over the evidence, "I did that."

Your mother grunted and lit another cigarette. "I can't imagine knowing her helped you much though."

My cheeks flushed, and I turned away, still examining the room. There were no pictures in the house. Not on the walls or the splintered mantle or the end tables. No sign of you anywhere. A knife twisted in my heart. This was supposed to answer my questions. This was supposed to make a difference.

Of course, there was somewhere I hadn't visited yet.

"May I see her room?"

Your mother led me down a hall into an 8x8 space with a bed, a pair of pale curtains withering on the windows, and not much else. "This is all she left behind, I guess."

You guess? I wanted to say, but I asked something else instead.

"Can I have a minute alone?"

Her penciled-in eyebrows twitched up, but then your mother glanced around, and apparently realizing there was nothing here worth stealing, she shuffled to the door. "I'll be in the kitchen."

Once she was gone, I searched everywhere for you. Under the bed, in the unlit corners, through the cobwebs in the closet. You'd left nothing behind. I crouched in the center of the room, waiting for you. Waiting for a sign of what to do next.

The hardwood floor was rough beneath me, and I leaned closer and pinched a piece of the grit between my fingers.

Salt. For a circle we'd cast together, so long ago nobody could recall it anymore.

And something else too. This close to the hardwood, I inhaled it now, so faint as to almost be forgotten. The scent of citrus. Pledge cleaner your mother used to scrub away our magic, over and over, probably admonishing you each time we did a spell, until there was no proof of what we'd done.

Now there was no proof of you either. You weren't here anymore. You hadn't been here for a long time.

I trudged back to the front of the house, defeat fizzling in my blood. "I appreciate your time," I said and slipped out the way I came in.

Your mother lingered in the doorway behind me. "Could you answer something for me?"

I turned back, my heart in my throat. "Yeah?"

Her eyes flickering with regret, your mother looked right at me. "What's my daughter's name?"

The question punched me in the gut. Instantly, I struggled to catch my breath, my knees threatening to give out beneath me, even as I searched for it, searched every memory I still had left. I hadn't spoken it in years, and it felt like a verboten word the moment it crossed my lips.

"Dahlia."

At once, your mother exhaled a long sigh, and something in her face twisted. "Thank you," she said, and closed the door.

The porch light went out, and everything in me seized up, as I finally understood.

I wasn't the only one who had forgotten.

Back at home, I went through every room. There were no photographs on the walls here either. No family pictures in any drawers. We'd been erased, everything in our lives wiped clean.

Half-dizzy with fear, I staggered up the stairs, back to the picture in my room, the only sign I'd found of us.

"Baby?" My mother materialized in the doorway, a greying terrycloth robe pulled tight around her waist. "What's wrong?"

I stared at her. "Who is she?" I asked.

"Everly," my mother said, "it's late. Not tonight, okay?"

"I can't wait anymore." I charged toward her, grasping for her hands, for her to just be close to me, just be honest with me. "Please."

Grimacing, she pulled away. "Don't do this."

"But she's from here, right?" My voice caught in my throat. "We grew up together?"

My mother nodded, not looking at me.

"Then tell me who she is."

"I can't remember." My mom spat the words at me and then immediately looked horrified with herself. "Neither can your father. We've talked about it. Over and over, every night."

I held perfectly still in the center of the room, doing my best not to scream, not to think of the next question I should ask. *Do you even remember me?*

But I didn't say it. I already knew the answer.

At my feet, all the Polaroids had redeveloped, our faces gazing up at me. I'd brought us back into being, our memories spilled across the carpet.

I gathered up the images. "There's something I need to do now."

My mom let me borrow the car.

"Good luck, baby," she said, even though I didn't tell her where I was going.

All the way back to the college, I could barely catch my breath. With the pictures on the passenger seat, we trickled through in bits and pieces now.

You and me and our teenage secrets, far more dangerous than the occult. The way we did everything we could to get out of that town. The way we succeeded, just not how we'd planned. Or at least not how I'd planned.

I'd brought something else too. Your tin can telephone. The metal was starting to rust out now, but that didn't matter. Even from the driver's seat, I could hear you there, your voice sweet as a sanctuary bell.

"Are you coming back to me, Everly? Please come back."

I gnawed my bottom lip and kept on driving.

The door at the end of a familiar hallway was unlocked. Nobody had stayed here since us. Word around campus was that it was haunted.

Our room. The only place you ever felt safe.

I kneeled in the middle of the floor. Although you had forbidden it, I was about to break the rule one last time. This séance for two, one with a single candle and no other magic except what we'd always held inside us.

"Show me," I said, speaking to you and to me, and my body rose up.

With my eyes closed, I clawed through the façade, through the years that separated us from ourselves. Tearing at it didn't feel the way I thought it would. I expected time to weigh like pounds of flesh in my hands. Instead, it was all satin and chiffon, pulling back veils I never knew were there.

Beneath it all, I found us.

On the day we met, before ghosts or witches or the monsters of the world held sway over us. Two girls, bullied and strange, meeting on picture day at school, the camera flashes almost blinding us, but still, we managed to see one another across a crowded gymnasium, sensing a shared power within us. Using that power with fire and salt and secrets I'd discovered in dusty books.

"They don't want us here," we'd said, so we decided to find a place we could be safe together.

The rapping of our fists inside the salt circle. The heat of our hands gripped together around the candle flames. You and me rising up and memories floating away from a town where we didn't belong.

"Someday, we'll forget them," we said, two girls' resolve so potent that it erased everything else. "We'll forget, and we'll never go back."

This was our agreement, the spell we'd cast, neither of us understanding what'd we done. We'd bound ourselves together. Where one went, the other forced to follow. For all these years, I'd thought you were haunting me. It turned out we were haunting each other.

At once, I flooded back into myself. Everything I'd had and everything I lost. I could remember me now.

I could remember you too. In the flicker of the dying flame, you stood in front of me, here and not here. A ghost and a girl, all wrapped into one, your face not a moment older since the day you had vanished.

Young forever. Safe forever. This was what you were offering me, what you'd been offering for years. This had been our plan all along.

"Lock the door, Everly," you said, "and stay here."

I gazed back at you. "I can't," I said, the weight of the words almost too much to bear. "Why don't you come with me instead?"

But your skin turned translucent again, and I knew what that meant. You wanted to remain in this place where nothing ever had to change. A stasis where we could always be kids and always be together, the two of us against the world.

You'd once feared I was leaving you behind, but that had never been true. Anywhere I went, I'd asked to take you too. You just didn't want to come with me.

"Please don't leave me again," you whispered.

I took your hand in mine, so much heavier than I remembered it. "I won't."

"Promise?"

"Promise."

This was an oath I would keep. I'd gotten myself back, which meant now I could offer something. A tithe for who we had been, for the promise I had made.

All those years ago, at that last séance, you'd taught me something—that a person didn't have to die to become a ghost.

Who I was, the girl that I'd been desperate to remember. I didn't need to carry every piece of her with me after all, just like I didn't need to carry you. Instead, I could do one better. I could let us both go, leave who we were in the past where we belonged.

I dropped the Polaroids to the floor and stretched the tin can telephone until the string was taut. Then I stepped back, my head tipped down, and waited.

"Are you there?" Your question thrumming inside the metal. "Everly?"

"I'm here." My voice on the other end. The ghost of me. "I've missed you."

You wouldn't be lonely anymore. With a room of your own to haunt—our room—this was everything you'd ever wanted.

It was what I wanted too, but the rest of me couldn't stay here. There were secrets left in the world, and they were mine to unravel.

I extinguished the candle and crossed the empty room that wasn't so empty anymore. Even from the doorway, I could hear us, our voices echoing back and forth in the tin cans, the two of us giggling inside a world that no one else would ever touch.

I looked back once and saw us there—all that we were and all that we'd shared together. For an instant, I seized up, ready to stay, ready to dissolve into time with you, but I knew I couldn't. Part of me got to be here with you now, and that had to be enough.

From the hallway, I smiled at the two of us, and then with everything aching in me, I let the door close. The latch clicked on the other side.

"Goodbye," I said, and behind me, our ghosts were finally home.

I still couldn't remember the day we met. It was a memory that should never have left me. I should have held onto it, cherished it like a prized heirloom, tucked it away for safekeeping.

After all, when a person made a mistake like this, they ought to remember what got them there.

There was no body to recover, no inquest on your behalf.

"She went of her own free will," everyone concluded, as though you were merely an ordinary runaway, and that was that.

Only you weren't really gone. None of my books ever told me this, maybe because nobody knew except me—that a person didn't have to die to become a ghost. You just needed to want it badly enough.

After you vanished, no one came to pick up your things. No parents or siblings or other next of kin. That meant I inherited everything of yours—your clothes and your turntable and your tin can telephone.

All night, I played your favorite records. "Season of the Witch" and "Peek-a-Boo" and "Lust for Life," anything that might coax you back.

"Can you hear it?" I asked the ceiling, and turned it up a little louder just to be sure.

Soon, this was all I did, sealed up in our room like a tomb, desperate to bring you back from beyond. I stopped bothering to head down to the cafeteria where the lunch lady still glared at me, or the shower where the other girls always inched a couple steps away, quietly terrified they might meet the same fate as you if they got too close. Robbie brought me pizza, but sometimes, I wouldn't even open the door when he knocked. Why bother? It hadn't gotten you and me very far the last time I unlocked that door and let in the world.

I stopped going to class too. It seemed pointless now. Besides, college had already taught everything we needed to know. I learned how to conjure ghosts, and you learned how to be one.

"Where are you?" I whispered over and over, but not even the walls creaked back.

#

They kicked me out a semester before graduation.

"We're sorry about what happened to your roommate," the assistant dean said, his owl eyes peering me across a cluttered desk. "But we all agree perhaps a leave of absence would be in the best interest all involved."

As in, the interest of everyone who'd reported a strange smell coming from my room and had thought that I'd actually died in there. It was just the pile of rotting pepperoni pizzas stacked waist-high in corner.

"We'll figure it out," Robbie said when I told him goodbye. He sounded sincere about it too.

Paint Box, Puzzle Box

The turning leaves whisper to each other sometimes:
...Of getting older
...Of creation
...Of children misled & artists ignored.

"They're as real as you and me. Listen to them when
they question the shifting color.
Gently.
Their hearts beat for a clear spot in the fog
The gathering shadows of a friend's departure.

PAINT BOX, PUZZLE BOX

BY D. T. FRIEDMAN

When I was a young reviewer just starting out, I received an ARC for a collection called **Dark Faith.** It was a horror anthology dealing with the intersection of faith, horror, race, and gender. Filled with tons of big name authors and authors who "breaking onto the scene," I was excited to dive in, because it was a high profile anthology, and maybe...maybe my review would get noticed, because of all the big names I'd be reviewing.

Ironically (or, perhaps, not), while I found most of those stories by the "big names" to decent (if forgettable), my favorite story was "Paint Box, Puzzle Box," by newer writer D. T. Friedman. I had never before — and haven't since — read such a beautiful story about Art and Death, *and upon re-reading it, my appreciation for it only increases. Friedman has since taken a long break from fiction to pursue a career in medicine; here's hoping they'll return to the writing world, and start creating a different brand of medicine.*

A n aspect of Death came to a great Artist, the most celebrated creator of beauty that had ever illuminated the face of humanity. It found him in his studio, blending a background on an immense canvas.

"It is time," said Death, and the Artist turned to face it.

"That can't be. I ain't old yet."

"It doesn't always work that way," said Death, "especially not with artists." It looked thoughtfully over the barely-begun mural. "It is a shame, though. I would have liked to see what this was to have been."

"It was going to be my masterpiece," said the Artist. "A whole world, full of love and hate and kindness and evil...." He looked up at Death, piercing it with eyes that could capture the vitality of existence and spread it on canvas with a paintbrush. "Give me time to finish. When my work is done, I'll go with you without so much as a grumble."

"How much time?" Death looked around the Artist's studio, at the stacks and stacks of unfinished paintings, each promising a taste of the pure delight that could be found in all his work.

"One year." The Artist clutched his brush in his fist, willing Death with all his might to give in to his proposal. "Give me one year, and I'll create the greatest masterpiece that has ever been gifted to this world."

Death stood for a few moments, contemplating the canvas as if it could already see the wondrous creation that the Artist promised.

"I have always loved your work," it said. "One year."

THE OLD FOLKS HAD THEIR EASELS SET UP IN FRONT OF THE pond that first warm day when spring started to tip into summer. Willows and flowers were already starting to bloom on the canvases, and the jars of water were muddy with the sludgy drippings of dunked brushes.

Unbidden, Carlisa's eyes jumped around, counting them. There was little Rose, and Martha, and James, and Ella, and... a flutter of panic surged through her before she saw the unoccupied easel. Leo wasn't missing; he was there across the duck pond, holding his paintbrush to the sky to compare the colors. Carlisa let out a breath. Everyone had survived the winter. She ran down the hill to greet them.

She had seen them for years on her way home from school, and then work. A little cluster of geezers, chattering in their sun hats in those precious days after the chill left the air and before the sun got too hot for them. Something about them called to Carlisa, and they were often the subjects of her sketches.

Leo had noticed her one day and waved her over to chat. The friendship they struck was easy and cheerful; the whole group had murmured appreciatively over her drawings and Ella had kissed her on the cheek with her purse-string lips. The next time she visited, Leo handed her a paintbrush and a small canvas that she set on her lap like her sketchbook. She never really liked working with paint, or even really with color, but Leo's gentle suggestions brought a new life into all of her work, not just the amateurish pictures that the squiggles of her brush left behind.

"Look deep," he'd say. "You gotta paint the whole depth of the object, not just the surface." He'd show her his own painting, a woman in the distance walking a dog that looked for all the world like it was wagging its tail.

"Don't just see the colors," he'd say. "Feel them."

"Smell the colors," teased James from the other side of him. "Taste them, eat them for breakfast and sleep with them at night!"

"Oh, you leave them alone, silly," said Martha. "Don't listen to him, dear, he's colorblind."

That got a laugh from everyone; James' paintings showed he was anything but.

Leo held a dab of green on the end of his brush, stared at it hard. Carlisa focused her attention there, too.

"Feel where that color comes from," he said, his voice low. "See it for what it really is."

Carlisa could have sworn the color changed to blend in with the grass before he smudged it onto his canvas.

"Did you see it?" he asked.

Carlisa felt her head nodding, but she couldn't take her eyes off the delicate green of the grass in his painting. It was perfect in hue and value, but felt...wrong somehow. As if the color had been tipped askew.

"Ain't this a world," Leo said.

WHEN DEATH ENTERED THE ARTIST'S STUDIO A YEAR LATER, A mural of incredible beauty and complexity awaited it. Images danced across the canvas, illustrating every imaginable aspect of human existence from birth to death and before and beyond. The composition was breathtaking; each tiny detail begged closer scrutiny even as it drew the eye to the next, and the next, and the next.

Death stood for hours, studying the Artist's creation. Eventually it realized how much time had passed and pulled itself away. There would be eternity to appreciate the masterpiece, but Death had a job to do. It called to the Artist to appear, praising his work with a choked-up voice that it barely recognized as its own.

But there was no answer to its summons; the Artist was nowhere to be found.

Death found the Artist's wife in the cramped apartment below his studio, stirring a kettle of stew over an open fire. The stones of the hearth were blackened with soot, and the room was filled with the clutter of daily life.

"Where is your husband?" Death asked. "We had an appointment, and he has disappeared."

"Don't be ridiculous," said the Artist's wife. "He's upstairs, working on his masterpiece." She ladled a spoonful of stew into a wooden bowl and dunked a chunk of bread into it. Death followed her up the rickety ladder to the studio and stood behind her as she looked around.

"He must have stepped out for a bit," she said after a moment. She held out the bowl. "Would you like some stew?"

Something about the woman's manner made Death very suspicious. He reached for the bowl, but took her hand instead. The woman shuddered, but did not flinch away.

"He did not step out for a bit," said Death, "and this ruse does not fool me. You know exactly where your husband is."

"You're mistaken," she said, and disappeared down the ladder.

Death watched her go, and didn't miss the quick glance she threw at the Artist's mural.

CARLISA WATCHED LEO CAREFULLY, STUDYING HIS TECHNIQUE and squinting to catch a glimpse of that moment when the color would shift out of phase at the tip of his brush.

Leo's paintings flowed with life and energy, at the same time organic and carefully orchestrated.

He'd direct her occasionally as she painted, sometimes fitting his leathery fingers over hers to demonstrate a brush stroke. The others gave her pointers too, and her paintings developed as her eye matured to the new medium. She often stayed long after her friends had given up for the day, lost in the strokes and the dabs of paint on her cardboard palette.

Sometimes she'd round the duck pond to stand in Leo's spot, trying for hours to see the world as he did.

DEATH WAITED FOR DAYS AND DAYS, BUT THE ARTIST DID NOT return. The Artist's wife and daughter took turns offering it food and drink, and chasing away the children who occasionally climbed the ladder to gawk at it and giggle.

Death passed the time as it waited for the Artist to return by studying the mural. As the weeks turned into months, it realized that as amazing as the mural was, there was not much to separate it from the Artist's other work. This could not be the masterpiece that he had promised. Death tried to feel anger at being cheated, but all it could really feel was loss.

"You have to eat something," said the Artist's wife. "At least drink some mead."

Death declined, and caught the longing glance toward the mural that she stole as she retreated.

Death returned to studying the mural with new eyes.

It was energetic and complex, as if it held a life of its own just beyond the painted surface. Death closed its eyes and reached out its hand. It was not entirely surprised when it met no resistance.

Death's first step into the mural was tentative, though as only one part of Death itself, the aspect that entered was expendable. It was not fear that checked its progress, but awe.

The mural was but a portal, a doorway into a world beyond. And in it there was love and hate and kindness and evil, everything the Artist had promised. And there was beauty and grace and ugliness and art and waste....

But no Artist.

THE DAYS KEPT WARMING, AND THE HUMIDITY BEGAN TO GET the better of Rose. She only showed up in the early mornings now, the brims of her straw hats umbrella-like and floppy.

"How do you see past that, dear?" asked Martha.

"I love it when the weather gets hot enough to bring out the big hats," said Rose. "More surface area to play with."

And her summer hats were certainly a sight to see, painted with scenes of forests and deserts, with fake flowers and ivy bunching from the crown. James lifted the front of the brim to grin into her face.

"Oh, there you are," he said.

Rose rolled her eyes and dabbed a yellow splotch of acrylic across his nose.

"Watch it, lady," James said with affection, and laughed with everyone else as he wiped mustard streaks onto his handkerchief.

Leo stole Rose's hat and replaced it with his own beige cap. The straw brim drooped nearly to his neck when he pulled it over his head, and the silk flowers bobbed in the breeze as he nodded to the rest of them.

"I can see just fine," he said and made a big show of walking straight into his easel.

Carlisa nearly fell over laughing.

THE ASPECT OF DEATH SPLIT ITSELF INTO MANY PARTS, AND together they scoured every corner of the world the mural revealed to them. The Artist was not hiding from them there, not even by darting into the areas that Death had searched and dismissed.

Death gathered all its parts into the original aspect and sat in a sculpture garden with a glass of lemonade. The Artist was not in the world of his birth, and he had not disappeared into this new world, no matter what his wife seemed to think.

It got up to walk around, passing welded amalgamations of steel scraps, stone drums, and a long bronze log with a half-hitch knotted into the middle. The world the Artist had created even had its own artists, and their work was as creative or cheap or obscure or thought-provoking as art could be in their own world.

It paused next to a sculpture of nested boxes and leaned over to see what was inside. Through the rainwater that had collected in the bottom of the center box, Death could see a tiny bronze fish that looked like it was swimming when the water rippled.

Death stood straight, feeling as if it had been struck in the back of the head. It looked at the museum that the sculpture garden surrounded and had to restrain itself from running across the lawn.

Just as it suspected, every painting in the gallery opened onto its own world.

Death split itself into an uncountable number of parts and sent them to explore the worlds that lay beyond the portals in the Artist's mural.

A STRANGER WEARING A BLUE BUSINESS SUIT APPROACHED Carlisa as she held up her brush, trying hard to make the color turn like Leo had shown her that June morning. It was now the height of summer, and the heat of the day had chased her friends back indoors for a few hours.

Carlisa's paintings and charcoals had improved drastically since that first spring. A small gallery in the city had slated her for a show later that year, and she was determined to bring the same life into her work as Leo seemed to breathe into his.

"I'm looking for a friend of mine," said the stranger. "An artist like you. I haven't seen him for years, but..." his eyes flicked over to the spot across the pond where Leo always stood, communing with his paintbrush, "...I heard he spends some time here in the summer."

The stranger's eyes were warm and his face was open, but something made Carlisa want to look into him the way Leo had taught her to look into the depths of her subjects. Something froze and boiled inside the man who stood before her, and she withdrew her gaze as if she had been burned.

"I'm sorry," she said. "The only other artists I've seen stay around the flower gardens at the other end of the park."

The stranger regarded her for a long moment, and his eyes found Leo's spot across the pond again.

"My mistake," he said. "I'm sorry to disturb you."

He turned to leave, and then he stopped, his gaze lingering over Carlisa's painting.

"It's beautiful," he said. "I haven't seen that kind of vitality in a painting since...in a long time."

As the stranger strode off to wander around Leo's spot, Carlisa couldn't help but think of the time when Leo had twitched his paintbrush toward one of the daisies on Rose's hat. The paint on the end of the brush turned as yellow as the center of the flower, and Leo had dabbed it into one of his own daisies on his canvas. The color was perfect, but felt sideways.

The stranger ambled off, leaving Carlisa to stare across the pond. She didn't tell Leo about the stranger the next morning, but she watched for him all day.

Leo went to his spot often, twitching his paintbrush at the sky. Carlisa wondered why the colors over there were so much more fascinating than the ones on their side of the pond.

It was as Death had feared: each part of itself returned with the same report. In every world they found artists, and the works of art all contained worlds of their own. And worlds within worlds within worlds, without discernible end.

The Artist was still nowhere to be found.

Even though it worried about the complexity of the maze the Artist was hiding in, Death couldn't help but smile. It riffled through its memories of the search, wave after wave of appreciation and awe washing over it as it remembered the wonders it had encountered.

More shades returned to the sculpture garden as the years wore on. Some of the more adventurous ones reported that they nearly lost themselves as they wandered deeper into the labyrinth. But there was no news until the last straggler made its way into the garden, pale as if it had split itself but glowing with excitement.

"I have found a sign of his passage," said the part as it merged with the rest. "I have sent a shade of myself to investigate."

THE BLUE-SUITED STRANGER APPEARED MANY TIMES THAT summer, thankfully after even the mornings became too hot for her friends to tolerate.

"He's an elderly man," the stranger explained. "A great artist. Dark of face, light of hair. He often wears a beige hat, and he has this habit of holding his paintbrush up in front of his eyes. You're sure you haven't seen him?"

"Why don't you believe me?" asked Carlisa. The stranger thanked her for her time and left to round the duck pond.

She stared at his retreating back and tried to see into the core of him. Suddenly something in her gaze shifted, and she could see only a concentration of cold silence, floating over the ground. She gasped, and her gaze shifted back. The stranger had reached the far side of the pond, headed toward Leo's spot.

Carlisa looked away and knelt to focus on a puffball dandelion. When she concentrated hard, she managed to shift her gaze again. The fuzz stood out in her vision, and all she could see was the life aching to burst out from the seeds at its root. It felt dizzy, unbalanced.

As if in a trance, she reached out her paintbrush and dabbed the grey-white onto its end.

Her gaze shifted back once more and she stared at the unsteady, ashy color at the tip of her brush for long minutes. When she managed to tear herself away from her woozy sense of triumph, the stranger had disappeared once again.

What was it about that spot?

Leo spent a lot of time there, sure, but so much that the stranger was drawn there like a dog following a scent? She left her canvas and paints where they were and rounded the pond.

There was nothing special about Leo's spot. She stood where the grass had flattened under his sandals and tried to at least tease out a difference in the colors, or in the patterns of the clouds in the sky. Nothing suggested even to her that her mentor stood there day after day, twitching his paintbrush at the trees.

Until her view shifted.

A riot of colors assaulted her eyes, in streaks and dots and swirls. They swam around her in a whirling haze, forming and reforming into strange shapes and hues she had never seen before. It was as if she had fallen into the visions of a kaleidoscope psyche, immersed in a tank full of swarming, tropical fish.

Something was wrong with its alignment. She couldn't think in a straight line or hold the ground beneath her feet.

No wonder the stranger knew Leo was here. This spot was a beacon of creativity, a celebratory proclamation of the existence of her mentor. Leo couldn't have known that it would attract such a frightening visitor.

Her mind reeling, she carefully reached out her brush to touch a swirl of bright yellow and eggplant. The colors came away from the chaos around her and she smeared them across the sky.

The chilling stranger would not find Leo, she promised herself. She would hide every change he made to this spot, until the stranger dismissed it as abandoned and moved on. And she would try to heal the wrongness she felt, try to correct the dizzy distortion until it felt right.

If Leo noticed, he never said anything. The stranger didn't approach her again.

THE SHADE RETURNED TO THE SCULPTURE GARDEN, discouraged.

"It was a dead end," it sighed. "I thought I had tracked him to a world deep within the labyrinth, and indeed it seemed as if he meant to lead me there. But the signpost where the trail led fell into age as I watched. The Artist has left it behind and moved on to hide somewhere else."

The shade merged with the rest of itself, and Death sat dejectedly on the knotted bronze log to think.

CARLISA PRACTICED ALL SUMMER WHENEVER THE HEAT OF THE sun drove Leo indoors. She learned the patterns he had created, their rhythm and flow, and did her best to blend every change he made into something that seemed like it had always been there. She straightened skewed diagonals, trued uneasy swirls.

And as she learned more and more, she came to realize that this was not just an artist's creation of beauty for the sake of beauty; bits of the beacon seemed to warp parts of time and space themselves. She learned to manipulate these aspects as well, weaving them through the creation that had become as much hers as Leo's.

And then she began to set a trap.

THE DAYS BECAME COOLER AS SUMMER FADED LATE. CARLISA'S elderly friends could stay longer and longer into the day. She invited them to display some of their own work in her upcoming gallery show, and they buzzed with excitement as they touched the colors of the turning leaves to their canvases.

Leo had begun staring off into space a lot, often pausing from his painting for long minutes. The others noticed, and Carlisa heard them whispering to each other sometimes.

Leo was getting older, they said.

But Carlisa saw where his gaze fixed, and felt a flush of shame whenever he looked over to his spot. How could she have presumed to correct her teacher's creation? But the blue-suited stranger had not found him, and she comforted herself with that thought.

"I had a wife," Leo said once, suddenly. Everyone looked over at him; he had never spoken of any family. "A wife and children and grandchildren. Beautiful." He sighed, shook his head. "Ain't this a world, though?"

No one said anything. James clasped his shoulder before turning back to his work, but only Carlisa noticed that Leo used a clean paintbrush to dab a tear into the sky of his own painting, favoring his garden with a soaking rain.

She stopped erasing the changes he made to his beacon. It was his, after all.

IF THE ARTIST HAD BOTHERED TO CREATE A FALSE TRAIL FOR IT to follow, Death decided, there must be more than one. A spaghetti tangle, perhaps, the better to confuse and mislead.

It journeyed through worlds at random, casting around for another trail. It left a shade of itself at the portals of each world to make sure it could find its way out again. It stumbled across many similar paths, but they all led to the same center locality. The starburst trail was the only sign of the Artist's passage.

It sent a part of itself down the trail again, unwilling to belive there was nothing special about that world at the center.

"Be sure," it told itself.

AN ELDERLY MAN SAT ON A PARK BENCH IN CARLISA'S PAINTING, his face mostly obscured by the fuzzy grey hair of the woman who was leaning down to kiss him. A pigeon stood next to him on the bench, leaning over to peck at the sandwich that they were both ignoring. Behind them was the rest of the park, full of life but blurred into a barely perceptible background. The original charcoal sat next to Carlisa on the grass, one of her first and favorite sketches.

It seemed flat and lifeless now, compared to its canvas copy. At Leo's instruction, she sat for hours with the lovers, thinking about them as if they were real people.

"Because they are real," Leo said. "They're as real as you and me. So you gotta find out who they are and how they live, and listen to them when they tell you."

So she sat and asked them every question she could think of, shifting in and out of that strange world that offered her dabs of color if she would only reach out her brush.

And suddenly, she felt them. The man was about to reach up and encircle his lover's waist with his arm, gently pulling her down into his lap so their hearts could beat against each other. The woman ached for intimacy. And Carlisa was no longer a painter but a child wiping at a steamy window, each dab of paint rubbing a clear spot in the fog until the scene behind was revealed. But the window was tipped to the wrong angle; it was so hard to balance the strokes.

The dusk was gathering purple shadows when she tore herself away. She vaguely remembered her friends' departure as the light faded, the faraway clatter of paints disappearing into baskets and easels loaded into drag-along frames. Only one easel still stood, canted on the uneven lawn, its canvas showing a man straining for an apple he just couldn't reach. She felt his desperate hunger as the tree teased him, raising and dropping its branches in the hot breeze.

A movement caught the corner of her eye and she shifted back into the real world. The blue-suited stranger had returned and was rounding the duck pond. Leo stood in his spot, his back to them both, oblivious to the approaching danger.

"No!" Carlisa shouted. She ran along her side of the pond, knowing she would not be able to reach him in time. Leo turned at the sound of her voice, just in time to see the branches of a weeping willow wrap around the stranger and stuff him through a gash that Carlisa had cut into the fabric of their world. It would dump the stranger far away in time and space, somewhere not even Carlisa would be able to find again. Her trap had worked.

Leo gave a wordless cry and ran with a speed that belied his age to the place where the stranger had disappeared. But the rift had healed itself after swallowing its prey, and Leo's gnarled hands met only the bare branches of the willow. Leo stopped pawing through the wooden curtain and dropped his head in defeat. Carlisa thought to call to him, but she could do nothing but stand frozen and watch her friend clutch the branches in his hands.

When at length he looked over to her, his eyes were old and empty of hope. Carlisa backed away and ran, leaving her paints spread on the lawn around the kissing lovers.

THE MESSAGE ARRIVED AT NIGHTFALL, PASSED IN WHISPERS FROM portal to portal between the Artist's renditions of Death in each world.

"Follow the trail, but beware the girl!" "Follow the trail, but beware the girl!" "Follow the trail, but beware the girl!"

The shade that Death had sent to investigate the starburst trail never returned.

IT RAINED ALMOST CONSTANTLY THE WEEK LEADING UP TO Carlisa's show, so she only saw her friends when they stopped by the gallery to drop off their work. Carlisa fussed with matting and framing, but as much as she occupied herself, she couldn't help but notice that Leo never stopped by. Ella brought one of his paintings when she visited and watched solemnly as Carlisa arranged it next to one of her early charcoals. Leo faced out of the monochrome sketch, holding a paintbrush aloft as if he were about to twitch a bit of color from the eyes of whoever stood before it.

"It's just a bad time for him," Ella said. "He'll be back soon, don't you worry."

But behind her comforting smile, Carlisa could see the set resignation of a woman who had watched her friends disappear over the years, one by one. Carlisa hugged her, swallowing back the lump in her throat.

"He'll be fine," she said, and tried to believe it. The stranger was gone, wasn't he? Leo was safe.

DEATH STOOD AT A DISTANCE FROM THE BEACON, REGARDING IT with curiosity and a little fear. This was where a part of itself had disappeared.

"I am," the beacon announced with its color riot. "I exist!" To Death, it said, "I am here."

Death began to search.

OPENING NIGHT AT THE GALLERY WAS EVERYTHING A YOUNG artist could have hoped for. People actually came, lured by the promise of beauty and cheap wine in clear plastic cups. Carlisa laughed as her friends posed pseudo-nonchalantly by their charcoal portraits, waiting to be recognized so they could launch into descriptions of their own paintings, displayed alongside.

She munched a handful of Triscuits. She watched visitors point at her work and lean in for a closer look. James passed by, Rose's enormous flowered hat bumping his shoulder as she held tightly to his arm.

"Success," James said with a wink, and the two of them disappeared back into the small crowd. Carlisa smiled, but looked toward the door for what must have been the hundredth time that night. Why didn't Leo come?

And then, as surely as she had felt the lovers' longing to hold each other, she knew he was already there. Excitement thrilled through her, and she cast her gaze around the room to find him. She saw Martha, jabbering animatedly to a woman with punk-dyed blue hair, and James and Rose chatting with another couple at the refreshment table. James was flirting shamelessly with the young woman; she played along, lapping up the attention. Ella stood alone in front of Leo's painting, a hand on her cheek and smiling wistfully.

Carlisa didn't find Leo until she shifted her gaze to the color world. There he stood in the corner, watching his friends enjoy themselves as if they were young again. If he noticed Carlisa watching him, he gave no sign. After a while, he nodded in contentment and slipped out of the gallery. No one looked up as he passed.

Carlisa threaded her way to the door to chase after him, but he had disappeared into the night. She tried to pierce the darkness with her eyes, but not even her shifted vision revealed which way he had gone. She had just given up when she felt a shiver of emptiness pass behind her.

The white-suited stranger didn't look up as he walked by, intent on the quarry that had left only minutes ago. Without a backward glance, Carlisa followed him into the night.

The stranger's steps were long and quick with purpose. Carlisa nearly ran full-out to catch up with him, her cork wedges thudding at the sidewalk like a panicked heartbeat. He didn't look up until she planted herself firmly in his path.

"I know who you are," said Carlisa, surprised that her voice didn't shake when she addressed him. The stranger stopped, focused in on her with such intensity that she fought the urge to back away.

"Ah," said the stranger. "The troublesome young lady. I've heard about you. Step aside, please."

The stranger tried to walk around her, but she did not give way.

"You can't have him."

He stopped again, tilted his head.

"I must have him," he said. "The universe is out of balance, can't you feel it?"

Carlisa nodded despite herself. The tilt, the uneasy wrongness of the color world.

"The Artist feels it too. He has been calling for me for a long time."

"I won't let you take him," said Carlisa. "I've set more traps, all around."

"Will you walk with me, young lady? I have a long-overdue appointment, and I'd prefer not to be late."

"You won't get anywhere near him."

"That may be," the stranger allowed, and started again on his way. Carlisa tried to block his path again, but it was clear that the stranger was done playing on her terms. Eventually she fell into step beside him, her mind whirling through arguments and plans. They walked through the streets in silence.

Leo stood among the streaks and whirls of his beacon, oblivious to their approach. He twitched his paintbrush impatiently at the colors around him, and they flowed and combined and rarified at his direction.

Carlisa ran over to him, leaving the stranger behind on the path, and stood between them. The stranger approached, unhurried.

"Don't worry," she told Leo. "He can't get you."

Leo's hand clasped her shoulder.

"I've painted them over," he said. "The traps were brave and clever. I don't remember teaching you how to make things like that."

Carlisa turned to stare at him, a tickle of desperation rising in her stomach.

"Why...?" she managed.

"When I reached the end of my life — a long time ago, child — I created a labyrinth where I could escape Death. I planned to disappear into it, just long enough so Death would stumble around lost, looking for me in there. Then I'd come back and spend as much time as I had left loving my family and creating a body of work that'd be worthy to be called my masterpiece."

"So what happened?"

Leo shrugged. "I got trapped. Death got pulled in, just like I planned, but I never accounted for how fast the maze would grow. Every turn I took trying to find the way back to my family, I just got myself deeper in, and the worlds just multiplied around me."

"By then," said the stranger, standing beside them, "so much time had passed that your family had passed into my realm."

Leo nodded sadly. "I left signposts as far out as I could safely travel in every direction and still find my way back here before the labyrinth multiplied. I shoulda known how fast it would grow. I shoulda known. Damn fool."

Carlisa grasped his arm protectively, lest the stranger tried to take him away while she stood there.

The stranger held out his hand.

"Well?" he asked.

Leo looked to Carlisa, who held onto him as if she were drowning.

"You can let go, Carlisa."

"But...."

Leo smiled sadly, shook his head. Looking into the core of him, Carlisa suddenly saw how very, very old he was. His gnarled hands, his comfortable wrinkles, the oak-dark softness of his skin and eyes...they all seemed tired, now that she really looked. Leo was weary, and he wanted his wanderings to end.

Carlisa swallowed hard, trying to think of something to say that would make him stay. Plea after plea swam through her mind, but she couldn't make herself speak. Leo wasn't asking her permission; he only wanted her acceptance. And he would leave without either.

Hating herself and determined not to cry, she slowly released Leo's arm. Leo kissed her forehead, then her cheek, then her hand, and then turned to join the stranger.

"Wait!" Carlisa managed before they left her. Leo turned back. "What about your masterpiece?"

"I'd already made it," Leo said. "I just didn't know it at the time."

"Can I see it?"

Leo smiled. "Yes, child. I think you can."

He motioned all around with an open hand, and Carlisa looked with the eyes that Leo had shown her how to use. And beyond the park she saw another world, and beyond that another, and another, and another. They bloomed before her, one from the other, each filled with love and hate and kindness and evil. As she watched, they shifted from their distortion and settled back into their proper alignment. They split off and nested into each other, universes and universes full of life.

When she came back into herself, Leo and the stranger had disappeared. The tears she had been holding back were spent on her cheeks, and she clutched Leo's paintbrush in her hands. Her chest was heavy and her throat felt choked closed, as if she would never speak again. She turned away from the beacon, now a monument, and slowly left the park.

She touched Leo's paintbrush to her cheek and swept it deliberately across the sky. A warm rain fell over the city as she made her way back to the gallery.

DEATH AND THE ARTIST WALKED SIDE BY SIDE THROUGH THE park as old friends who had not seen each other for too long.

"I saw myself everywhere in your work," said Death. "I would have thought you'd avoid me as much as possible."

"You can't have beauty without balance," said the Artist. "It just doesn't work that way. Especially not with artists."

"These worlds that you've created," said Death. "They are all so beautiful." It picked a sprig of gladiola, held it up to the light of a streetlamp. "This in itself is a masterpiece," he said. The Artist laughed. "What?"

"This world," said the Artist, a gleam of almost paternal pride in his eyes, "it ain't even a one of mine."

"Whose is it?"

"No idea. Ain't it a world, though?"

"Sure is."

Together, they disappeared into the darkness.

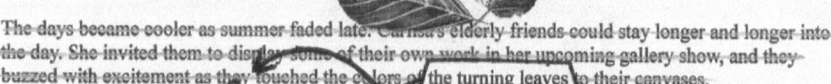

The days became cooler as summer faded late. Carlisa's elderly friends could stay longer and longer into the day. She invited them to display some of their own work in her upcoming gallery show, and they buzzed with excitement as they touched the colors of the turning leaves to their canvases.

Leo had begun staring off into space a lot, often pausing from his painting for long minutes. The others noticed, and Carlisa heard them whispering to each other sometimes.

Leo was getting older, they said.

But Carlisa saw where his gaze fixed, and felt a flush of shame whenever he looked over to his spot. How could she have presumed to correct her teacher's creation? But the blue-suited stranger had not found her, and she comforted herself with that thought.

"___," Leo said once, suddenly. Everyone looked over at him; he had never spoken of any ___ and children and grandchildren. But ___ shook his head. "Ain't this a ___

___ anything. James clasped his shoulder ___ turning back to his work, but only Carlisa ___ used a clean paintbrush to dab a tear into the sky of his own painting, favoring his garden ___ king rain.

She ___ erasing the change he made to his beacon. It was his, after all.

\#

If the Artist had bothered to create a false trail for it to follow, Death decided, there must be more than one. A spaghetti tangle, perhaps, the better to confuse and mislead.

It journeyed through worlds at random, casting around for another trail. It left a shade of itself at the portals of each world to make sure it could find its way out again. It stumbled across many similar paths, but they all led to the same center locality. The starburst trail was the only sign of the Artist's passage.

It sent a part of itself down the trail again, unwilling to believe there was nothing special about that world at the center.

"Be sure," it told itself.

An elderly man sat on a park bench in Carlisa's painting, his face mostly obscured by the fuzzy grey hair of the woman who was leaning down to kiss him. A pigeon stood next to him on the bench, leaning over to peck at the sandwich that they were both ignoring. Behind them was the rest of the park, full of life blurred into a barely perceptible background. The original charcoal sat next to Carlisa on the grass, one of her first and favorite sketches.

It seemed flat and lifeless now, compared to its canvas copy. At Leo's instruction, she ___ with the lovers, thinking about them as if they were real people.

"Because they are real," Leo said. "They're as real as you and me. So you ___ out and how they live, and listen to them when they tell you."

So she sat and asked them every question she could think of, shifting in and out ___ that offered her dabs of color she would only reach out her brush.

And suddenly, she felt them. The man was about to reach up and encircle her ___ gently pulling her down into his lap so their hearts could beat against each ___ for intimacy. And Carlisa was no longer a painter but a child wiping at a steamy ___ rubbing a clear spot in the fog until the scene behind was revealed. But the window ___ the inside angle, it was so hard to balance the strokes.

The ___ gathering purple shadows when she ___ herself away. She vaguely remembered her friends departure as the light faded, the faraway clatter of paints disappearing into baskets and easels

Buckeye Jim in Egypt

Stay quiet.
Some of you don't know death like I do.
This is my job: to be the child of a bullet,
A bone-rivened roar of thunder
In all the days to follow.

BUCKEYE JIM IN EGYPT

BY MORT CASTLE

To this day, Mort Castle's novella Buckeye Jim in Egypt is still one of my favorite stories about the everlasting power of faith in mankind. So often — wrongly so, I believe — religious stories lean overly hard into the depravity of man, and how the only thing that makes us worthy is our faith in God. However, the beautiful thing about Castle's tale is he flips the narrative: It's God's faith in us — despite our faults and capacity for violence and hatred — which makes life beautiful. A powerful sentiment, regardless of your faith or denominational practice.

Note: Because this story takes place during a time high racial tensions, and accurate portrayals of racists have

been made, racial slurs have been used by certain characters as extensions of their real personalities. Be advised.

PROLOGUE

In the beginning, there was darkness.
Then came light.
That is the beginning of everything.

I

The more mundane among us contend Southern Illinois is called "Egypt" or "Little Egypt" because of its southernmost town, Cairo, on the Mississippi River.

More probable is that the term came into usage because we are still waiting for a Moses to lead us out of here right to the Promised Land, although every time one appears on the scene, we kick him flush in the backside and tell him to let us tend to our own affairs.

—Brian Robert Moore, weekly columnist,
1920-1973, "I'll Tell You What!" for the
Sesser Sentinel, Eads St. Publications,
Sesser, Illinois

Way up yonder, above the sky,
white bird nests in a green bird's eye.

"Buckeye Jim" An American folk song,
usually performed on the banjo

Monday, July 12, 1925

SOMETIMES HE FORGOT WHO HE WAS.

Sometimes he forgot what he was doing here.

It was just past 7:30 in the morning, and already the thermometer had hit a swampy 80, but it was not the temperature or fatigue that caused the man in the light weight suit coat to set down his straw valise and banjo case and lean on the rail of the half-mile long bridge. He needed to think. Gazing down at the rippling, sun reflecting waters of the Washauconda River helped to bring about a mind calming focus.

He reached into his pocket. He found it: a lucky buckeye. Every time he reached into his pocket, there would be one— and one only. The seed of the horse chestnut was brown and brittle; it felt as though there were something magical and off-center within it. It was exactly like the world.

His smile came slow and easy. Nobody would ever mistake him for handsome, but when he smiled, it made most folks like him.

He knew who he was.

He was Buckeye Jim.

This time.

He knew what he had to do.

Buckeye back in his pocket, he hoisted his grip and banjo. Just then a new, deep green, Oakland All American Six pulled up, the powerful Phaeton model. Of course, in this weather, the windows were down. The driver, in a straw fedora, tie knotted in a half-Windsor, a prominent American flag pin on his collar, leaned toward Buckeye Jim. "How do."

"How do," Buckeye Jim answered, bending down, face framed by the window. "Your automobile is a beaut."

"I do thank you. Might I offer you a ride into Ft. Lorraine? I assume that is your intended destination."

"Yes, sir, " Buckeye Jim said.

"The Devil is always hiring fiddlers and banjo pickers in hell, but if you're after employment in the mines, Mr. June Legrand's got a one hole privy operation in Ft. Lorraine that is likely to oblige. If you don't mind working next to niggers. And if you don't mind being forced to join the union."

Buckeye Jim said nothing as he stowed his gear in the back.

The driver added, "Not saying Legrand's a Bolshevik. Not saying he's a nigger lover. I do wonder if he's a true-blue American."

The auto felt massive. Buckeye Jim wondered if he would ever get used to cars. He did enjoy the smell of new cars. He liked the smell of gently flowing rivers and hot sun on steel bridges…

He suddenly remembered the strong and surprising odor of light, a smell that was itself pure radiance, shattering and banishing the darkness.

The driver's name, said the man who wore his nation's flag on his collar, was Mark E. Dupont. ("Thank you for the ride, Mr. Dupont, and people call me Buckeye Jim.") He seemed a friendly fellow, not too jolly or too serious.

Not too much one or the other… He could be a dangerous man, Buckeye Jim reckoned. On several occasions, Buckeye Jim had been killed by just this sort of man.

Mark E. Dupont casually mentioned he was assistant superintendent up to the new strip mine owned by Illinois Coal and Power north of Herrin. A new process, strip mining would be the wave of the future, and it was swell. It meant more profit for everyone. Also, Mark E. Dupont mentioned (casually), he'd been elected to Herrin's town council. There had been talk—casual, but who could tell— about his running for mayor.

He started to say something else casual when Buckeye Jim said, "Sure a fine automobile. A real ace."

Dupont chuckled. "Well, I would have been most happy and satisfied with just your standard model, but my boys would not have it."

"You have sons?" Buckeye Jim asked.

Dupont said, "Well, I do have a family, and I do have boys. Two boys, a girl, and a fine, Christian wife who dotes on me.

"But I was not referring to my off-spring. I meant the boys in the Klan."

"Clan," Buckeye Jim said quietly.

There were times when his mind became a tedious and troublesome thing.

So many memories ...

He did remember clans. The MacEldoes? The McCutcheons? In Scotland. He recalled Scotland as a land of thistles and foggy mornings more gray and ominous than anywhere else on earth. *And cutting through the grayness, he could remember the swirling-squeal of the pipes, eerie and mysterious, a summons to war and death...*

He remembered ...

"... I'm the leader. What you call a Cyclops," Dupont said. "'Course they have to inflate it some, call me the 'Grand Exalted Cyclops' and what not." Mark E. Dupont sounded like he didn't mind that "his boys" wanted him to be "grand" and "exalted" and to drive a Phaeton.

"Well, I don't know," Buckeye Jim said.

"A lot of people don't know," Dupont said, "and among 'em is one Mr. C. Cooper Legrand, Jr. I'll be jawing some with him today. Rich man like him, what he can't realize is this was hard-crabble, bare bone, poor country 'fore the mines come. And if all the really big companies from out east choose to leave because Legrand has a head full of foreign thinkin' and a heart that beats pure nigger time like a shufflin' pickaninny ..."

Buckeye Jim said nothing. He was confused. Not infrequently, people thought him dull-witted.

But if you live many lives, and you don't know what you should know and you do know what you shouldn't know... My, oh, my, and wasn't it a perplexing business?

Mr. Dupont was talking about—

"... the Klan is four-square for the Bible. I'd imagine a right-looking American fellow such as yourself, why, you wouldn't be having any moral or spiritual argumentations with that, would you, Mr. Buckeye Jim?"

With all his poor head had to tote, sometimes Buckeye Jim felt he had no room left over for a sense of humor, but doggone! That did make him laugh!

"Mr. Dupont," he said. "I would testify in any court of the land or on Judgment Day that I have no dispute with the Bible."

"Well, good, good," Mr. Dupont said. He went on to tell how the Ku Klux Klan defended Americans from foreigners and Communists and Catholics (especially those "Eye-talian Catholics but also Bohunk and Polack" Catholics), and he went on to tell how it brought true Christianity to those as needed the Gospel Truth, and he went on to tell how it put the fear of God in the bootleggers, like those East St. Louis Shelton Brothers, or that Jew Charlie Birger with his road house, the Shady Rest, and he went on and he went on and on and on ...

Buckeye Jim said, "Looks like we're here."

Like virtually all Southern Illinois town squares, Ft. Lorraine's was a circle. In the center, an imposing island of civic sanctity, stood the municipal building, new red brick, with broad, white concrete steps. Merchants on the town's center hub included Walker and Sons clothing, the Vick-Cline Pharmacy (where the forty cent size Fletcher's Castoria was on sale for twenty-nine cents), and Ulricht's Shoe Store.

Buckeye Jim got out and pulled his gear after him.

"Good luck," Dupont said, shaking his hand through the passenger window portal. "You find Ft. Lorraine isn't exactly to your liking, that maybe it smells too niggery, you come on up north of Herrin way and perhaps I can do you some good."

"Why, thank you," Buckeye Jim said. You know, Buckeye Jim felt altogether humorous today. "Mr. Dupont, you are the very first Grand Exalted Cyclops I have met in my entire life and I am likely some older than you take me for."

Mark E. Dupont waved a "Pshaw" hand in pleased self-deprecation.

"And by the way," Buckeye Jim said, "I'm a Jew."

II

With Britain's defeat of France in 1763, the dreams of a French empire in Illinois ended. In the south of the state, such lasting place names as Vincennes, Prairie du Rocher, Bellefontaine are usually so mispronounced in southern Illinois twang as to be unrecognizable to any Frenchman.

But today, in Ft. Lorraine, Illinois, in Union Grove County, "an experiment in planned living" is being conducted that makes many of the local citizenry proclaim their community "a heaven on earth."

The "social scientist" responsible is C. Cooper Legrand, Jr., who owns the Old Legrand and Washauconda River Mining Corporation, one of the smaller operations in the region—"but one of the safest," Legrand stresses. A childless widower, C. Cooper Legrand is usually addressed good-naturedly by his employees as "June," or "Juney." With enthusiastic forthrightness, he states, "Yes, we are working together to create a utopia, an earthly paradise if you will. After all, my father created hell."

In addition to owning the mines, the Legrand family built and owns much of the town of Ft. Lorraine itself, renting living quarters to its laborers. But these houses are a far cry today from what they were in "the not so good old days." According to the Illinois Coal Report for 1898, these dwellings "lacked central heating and running water. One outhouse privy served six homes. Workers led 'joyless, brutal, dangerous lives,' and had little opportunity to 'even dare to dream of bettering themselves.'"

"My father died in 1910, and I bear him no grudge, and I hope others do not. He was not cruel, merely unenlightened," states Legrand. "I was 22 at his passing, and I felt myself ready. I had studied in Europe, in France, England, and Germany. I had visited Russia. I knew that if capitalism did not change, it would be brought down, that there would be a revolution in blood and fire. History would condemn those who reaped inhumane profits from the sufferings of the masses. I envisioned a decent, compassionate capitalism, one that has at its root the understanding that the human experience is one we all share."

Upon assuming the mantle of leadership, Legrand immediately instituted new safety features in the mining operations, and transformed the workers' "squalid huts" into real homes. He opened negotiations with the United Mine Workers of America and his operations today are 100% union.

Not infrequently, C. Cooper Legrand, Jr. is asked if he is a "leftist," or even a Socialist or Communist, and in this part of the country, these are damning labels.

But Legrand laughs at such allegations of "Un-Americanism." "What I am is a progressive," he maintains.

"I believe in people. I'm working for a better world for all of us, without the invisible walls that have kept people apart for too long."

> *From "Utopia in Illinois?", a feature*
> *article by Roy L. Potts, St. Louis Tribune-*
> *Leader, May 10, 1924.*

"Horsehit."

> *Mark E. Dupont, Grand Exalted Cyclops*
> *of the Knights of the Ku Klux Klan; a private*
> *response to the above article.*

The Knights of the Ku Klux Klan stand for the purest ideals of native-born, white, Gentile four-square Americanism:

The tenets of the Christian religion.

The protection and nurturing of white womanhood.

The freedom, under law, of the individual.

The "right to work" of the American working-man; his individual liberty to enter into such business negotiations and private and personal contracts as he chooses.

> *From a two color handbill entitled "The Fiery*
> *Cross: America's Guiding Light," written by*
> *Mark E. Dupont andt he Rev. James E. Scurlock,*
> *January, 1924*

"Horsehit."

> *C. Cooper Legrand, Jr., in a private response*
> *to the above quoted handbill, prior to his*
> *ripping it to pieces as he laughed.*

III

H e liked it.

By that afternoon, he'd walked here and he'd walked there, and after a time, he knew Ft. Lorraine was the right place.

A little girl on the east side sold him a one penny lemonade, ferociously cold and snapping with lemon.

He saw a blue-jay.

A negro woman on the front porch of a neat little house in a neighborhood of neat little houses called to him.

"Sir?" She held her little boy by the hand, a child of perhaps five or six.

Buckeye Jim went up the walk. He liked the way she sounded, not the "hiding away" voice black folks often use for white people.

"You lost?"

No.

No one is lost; no one is forsaken, were the words that came to his mind.

There were flowers in the yard. Impatiens. Pink and yellow roses. And tulips. July, and so hot, and yet the tulips were still here and lovely.

A happy perplexity filled his head, and he felt a small grin growing that he knew to be silly. Maybe at last, at last, it was coming around! Coming around here, in Ft. Lorraine, and maybe this town would be a light unto the nations…

He was, he said, just sort of scouting the territory, and he told her his name.

She was Mrs. Willoughby. Her little boy was Paulie Jason. The child drew closer to her. "My Paulie can't talk. He can hear, but he can't talk. Doctors don't know as to why it is."

Buckeye Jim put his small straw suitcase down on the walk. He reached into his pocket. "Yes! I thought I had me one. And it's an extra special lucky one!"

A snap of thumb launched the buckeye. At the top of its arc, it hung there …

… and there it hung −

Then Paulie Jason let loose his momma and slowly, slowly, his hand swam out as the buckeye dropped through weighted depths of air to land on his palm and his fingers closed over it.

Buckeye Jim turned and walked away.

Paulie Jason said, "Goodbye, Mr. Buckeye Jim."

IV

Socialism, communism, and other doctrines have played no part in the violence and murder which have brought such ill fame to the "queen of Egypt."

William L. Chenery in The Century

... respect to Mr. Chenery, this self-proclaimed Sage of Sesser holds that we are just as willing to kill for doctrines as your most radical, bearded, bomb-toting, Eastern European anarchist. Many of our law enforcement officials and politicians are willing to kill for the doctrine, "Under the Table and in My Palm," while our bootleggers resort to violence to enforce the "Right of Americans to Get Drunk." Our Kluxers, of course, will take up arms in defense of every town's prerogative to conduct festive lynching bees, while I personally know at least two Methodist churches whose congregations load the cannons if you try to take away their covered dish pot luck dinner, which they hold as a sacrament.

Of course we Egyptians, when we lack doctrines to kill for, will quite happily kill because A) we've nothing more interesting to do and B) our nation expects us to act like savages.

Brian Robert Moore, "I'll Tell You What!"

Son of a bitch! Mark E. Dupont, THE Grand Exalted Cyclops, did not hold with unnecessary violence, but at this particular instant, he could violently put a new Montgomery Ward steel-toe work boot all the way up that man's ...

Mr. C. Cooper Legrand, Jr., "Call me June," trying to be "plain folks," but oh, the man was just so full of himself!

Talk reason to him. That's what the Illinois Coal and Power Company wanted its designee (and rising member of the management team!), Mark E. Dupont to do.

Illinois Coal and Power would like Legrand to sell them his enterprise. Not that Legrand was real competition, not with I C and P's far cheaper strip mining process and non-union operation ...

—But I like having a coal mine, Mark! It's fun!

Negotiations could begin immediately. Accommodations could be reached with the union. Mr. Legrand could play a role on a board of directors ...

Mr. Legrand, whether you know it or not, there was trouble stirring; many of Egypt's citizens did not hold with white and colored living and working together like that—

—Mark, when they came off their shift, all you see is eyes, so you can't tell a colored coal miner from a white one!

—this union thing, well, in the long run, it might DE-stroy individual incentive...

—meant no one was cheated and everyone got what was coming to him. Do unto others and all that, Mark ...

(Like to give you what's coming to you! Like to do unto you until you're done for certain, chucking Bible at me when nobody ever sees you at church!

(Hmm, could be some of the fancy learning you got overseas included how to spurn the Lord your God? You an atheist, Juney-Bug? By the way, how long your wife's gone and you still single and no lady around but that giant mammy house-keeper? Could be you more of a Jane than a June, Mr. Legrand?)

At sunset of a frustrating day, Dupont pulled up in front of his home in Herrin. If Dupont had been able to get things moving right, he'd been virtually promised the super's position at the Illinois Coal and Power's Ft. Lorraine mines!

But…

Say, what the hell?

He picked it off the seat of his new Oakland All American Six Phaeton.

A buckeye.

That guy this morning, that sort of mush brain …

The buckeye felt damn bad, he thought.

That's when lightning hit.

Lightning did not blast down from the heavens.

It burst from deep within him, and he felt the searing anguish in his eyes, felt his blood boil, felt his heart blaze and burn and turn to hard, black coal. And he felt a hellish hand wrap around his soul and squeeze!

The power of it threw him against the car door with enough force to spring it. He did a back somersault, losing his hat in the process. He pushed himself up to his hands and knees.

"Aaaaah! Aaaaah!" he shrieked, but it was a thin shriek, all breath and tightness. Jesus! Jesus!

Save me!

In spiritual and physical agony, his American flag collar-pin falling into the disgusting Niagara as he vomited and vomited...

... in the fetid black and green foaming spew from his guts, he could see incredibly tiny frogs, obscenely clean and shining eyed ... The Devil had him! He could not doubt! The Devil ...

In his anguish, he comprehended it. The Devil could don many guises ...

Buckeye Jim! Oh Lord, deliver me, Dupont begged, for The Devil has laid his fiery hands upon thy servant!

Somehow, somehow, Legrand, atheist nigger lover **DEVIL WORSHIPER!** had arranged it all. He understood that without any evidence but the revelation of his tormented spirit.

Dupont staggered to his feet, slumped against the car. A sudden cramp, and drool and frogs—he could feel them on his tongue and palette!—leaked out of his mouth down his clothes.

Up at his house, he heard the commotion. "What is it? What?!?"

What it was was he was DAMNED!

He lurched into the car.

He needed God's help.

"Please, God, please..." he whispered. The automobile jerked away, as he squinted to see through his tears.

He had to get to Granny Gunger!

Give me that old time religion!
It's good enough for me!

GRANNY GUNGER HAD A REGAL AND HIDEOUS DEMEANOR AS she presided at the rickety table in her hovel out near the tracks at Whittington Curve, a prime location because, when a train slowed for the turn, coal would tumble from the tender and she'd reap the bounty of Luck and the Illinois Central Railroad.

Granny Gunger came from the hills. She knew dowsing and how to draw fire out of wounds. She could stop bleeding or set bones. She could not re-grow an eye, however, and so there was the mucus and muscle rippling empty socket where her drunken father had accidentally thumbed her when all he'd meant to do was punch her.

"You stink, Mister Dupont. You stink like you crawled up a OH-possum's ass," Granny Gunger said. Granny Gunger was known for plain speaking.

Dupont told her why he'd come.

"Frogs," she said. "Frogs is bad. You got strong enemies doin' Satan's bidding. Mister Dupont, the Old Deceiver wants you. You're in sorry shape now, and I don't think you'll like eternity in hell much better."

"Help me, Granny!"

"You got faith, Mister Dupont? You got true faith and the courage of it?"

"Yes."

"You got a RE-solve for God A'mighty to put you to the test?"

Dupont shivered. "Yes," he whispered.

"You got five dollars?"

He nodded.

Granny Gunger slouched over to the black box, unfastened the chain, opened the padlock and reached in. Mark E. Dupont prayed as he had never prayed before.

At just under three feet, Sweet Mercy was not the biggest diamond back rattlesnake in the universe, but he was a lovely one, with radiant coloring and perhaps the snakiest eyes ever to grace the mean triangle of a rattler's head.

Granny Gunger kissed Sweet Mercy right at the bony ridge of his nose.

Sweet Mercy rattled happily.

"They shall take up serpents," Granny Gunger quoted scripture. Then she improvised, as she hobbled to Dupont. "For if they be a generation of vipers, what profiteth a man to dwell far from the tabernacle as he goes up to the Land of Goshen?"

Mark E. Dupont thought, prayed, and entreated the Lord.

"Pucker up now," Granny Gunger said. "Let the kiss of salvation come to you."

Dupont closed his eyes. He puckered. He heard Sweet Mercy's rattle. He felt the snake's subtle breath—sugary, like the breath of a baby.

Then Sweet Mercy's forked tongue flicked against the dry, chubby, pursed lips.

Dupont flew to the floor, landing on his heels and the back of his head.

And when he could rise, he did not doubt.

He knew it—because he FELT it! HALLELUJAH!

Free! Saved! Praise God!

Delivered! he thought, as Sweet Mercy got delivered back to his box.

"Now, Mister Dupont," Granny Gunger said, "we got to do us some plannin'! We got to take some precautionary actions. We got to make sure. We must confound your enemies."

"Yes."

"I got somethin' special," Granny Gunger said. "It's got night-shade and a bloody thorn and the lips and eggs of a stone blind fish in it."

"What does it do?"

"You'd best believe it does just fine."

After Dupont's departure—preceded by her reminding him of the five dollars he owed her—Granny Gunger sat with Sweet Mercy in her lap, petting the diamond back like a tabby. "Well," she said, "told him the Old Deceiver wanted him, and now the Old Deceiver's got him."

She laughed.

"Don't you?"

Sweet Mercy rattled in a way that sounded almost exactly like Granny Gunger's laugh.

V

Prior to beginning another insightful commentary on our ever interesting Egypt, I wish to thank those who have been kind enough to write the Sentinel comparing me with Mr. H. L. Mencken, and offering to tar and feather us both as soon as we can find the time for this singular honor. While I greatly admire Mr. Mencken's writings, I find him far too optimistic about the future of the allegedly human race.

Now, let's talk about the pride of Egypt: A true crime lord. With the passing of the years, it becomes more and more difficult to distinguish Charlie Birger from the "legend of Charlie Birger."

I knew and liked Charlie. On occasion, I bought him an illegal beer at his illegal road house, and he bought me one. We told one another jokes, few of which could be printed in this newspaper.

As his acquaintance, then, I will tell you I do not believe that the shady owner of Shady Rest rode the rodeo circuit with Tom Mix, but I have seen him on horseback and cannot doubt his formidable skills.

I do not believe that, following an argument in a St. Louis speakeasy, Charlie fought to an impromptu bloody draw with Jack Dempsey, but I believe he would go to the line against anyone of any size because I have seen him do just that.

More folks liked Charlie than not, and they had reason. The poor of Harrisburg knew his charity. A good number of men found employment, if not necessarily of the legal variety, because of Birger. He had wit, grace, and courage. He was a man's man, and on occasion displayed a streak of sentimentality that would have been derided in a less masculine fellow.

Above all, Charlie Birger was the steadfast friend.

If Charlie liked you, he'd kill anybody for you.

Brian Robert Moore, "I'll Tell You What!"

Tuesday, July 13, 1925
A SLOW AFTERNOON AT SHADY REST, SO, NOTHING MUCH ELSE to do, the boys wanted to see him shoot. Charlie felt frisky and in the mood. They went out back, behind the pole barn.

Though a Tommy was his weapon of choice these days—you had to stay modern and keep up with competition, to say nothing of your enemies!—he took his old Winchester. The boys tossed beer bottles and he snapped off shots from the hip: Eight shots, eight hits.

"That's the way it is done by a shootist, ole hoss," Charlie said. Born in New York City, Charlie Birger spent his youth in the west as a cavalry soldier, a wild horse breaker, a gambler and a gun-fighter, and he still often spoke the palaver of the range. It had been a good life out there; folks played you straight. You were what you were, what you said, and what you did, and that was all that counted.

Here in Egypt, well, let's just say it was considerable different. You couldn't count on all the cards being on the table. But Charlie had done well; they called him the "King of Egypt."

Now the King needed a suitable chariot.

So after a beer, Charlie and some of the boys drove off to West City, where Joe Adams, mayor, gin-mill owner, and proprietor of a Stutz dealership, was working on a new conveyance for His Royal Majesty!

BUCKEYE JIM GOT HIRED BY THE OLD LEGRAND AND Washauconda River Mining Corporation.

In the weeks following this uncelestial event, there were other happenings that might be viewed as more interesting or even "curious."

One of them involved K. J. Pritchard. One afternoon, when, as usual, he was standing on the square, dark glasses and a tin cup, a cardboard sign around his neck saying—

A VETERAN
I WAS BLINDED FOR LIBERTY'S SAKE

—he sensed someone standing in front of him. He said, "The big war. I was in the big one."

"I was in that one, too."

"It was gas. They didn't have to gas us! It was NOT FAIR!!!"

"Nothing ever is, not in war."

"Help me?"

K. J. Pritchard heard something drop into the tin cup. It didn't sound like a coin. Cheap bastard.

With his left hand, he took it out. It felt like... It felt like a buckeye!

He held it up. Yes, that was just what he was looking at, a...

He ripped his dark glasses off, shattered them on the pavement.

The bright sunlight burning his eyes, he wept.

THERE WAS A CAR WRECK LATE ONE NIGHT OUT PAST CRENSHAW Crossing. A rattle-trap Ford full of young boys and younger girls who were full of shine. In the moonlight, you could see the silvery white of bone punching through flesh, and a head squashed the way you'd swear a head couldn't be squashed, and a bloody mess in which you could not tell twisted metal from human meat.

One of the victims, 15 year old Anna Beulle Diggs, would later say, "I had this strange dream. I heard a voice, kind of like Daddy when he's disappointed and angry both. It said, 'This is foolish, but children ought not to die for being foolish. So all of you, you live. And sometimes you think about just how precious life is.'

"Well, we all did live. Maybe it was plain luck, but such a great big lot of luck like that might be a miracle. I think, anyway...

"I don't know why I've kept it, but when they found us, I had this buckeye in my hand, and I have had it as a lucky piece ever since."

IT WAS HEAVY DARK, THE FROGS AND CRICKETS AND NIGHT sounds, loud, so loud in his throbbing head. Out in front of The Jolly Sports road house, Sam Washington had a gun and no options. With just the one arm, the other blown into sausage in the explosion at the fireworks factory where he had worked, he couldn't find a job, not anymore. He was colored and he couldn't read and he was as tapped out as a man could get.

Once he'd been a pretty good gut-bucket piano player. Not a real professor like Jelly

Roll or Willie The Lion, or even the white boy, Art Hodes, but he might have had the makings of a tickler. He used to dream, one arm ago, of going to New York and making records and playing for the swells, just like Mr. Jelly Lord.

Once he had a dream and now he had a gun.

Then there was a white man standing in front of him. He seemed to pop up just like a haunt, but his smile was a man's.

"Mr. Washington, let's make a trade. Let's swap death for life. You give me the pistol. I give you…"

Washington knew it was all right…The man said, "Now what you do is take your dream and go on and live it. Play the piano, Mr. Washington."

"I don't know, sir. You need ten fingers to play piano."

"How many you got?"

"Five."

"So move the five twice as fast."

… STRANGE REPORTS THAT NONE OTHER THAN JESUS, FORMERLY of Nazareth, is paying a visit. Call me a doubting Thomas, but I fear our Egypt an unlikely locale for the Second Coming. Our civic minded Kluxers (and clucks!), enforcing the Volstead Act, will not tolerate His turning water into wine, the unions will move if He attempts to practice His carpentry without getting a card, and few of our churches will listen for five seconds to this "foreigner's" ludicrous doctrines of compassion, charity, and tolerance.

Brian Robert Moore, "I'll Tell You What!"

Tuesday, August 17, 1925
First Shift at Old Coop #3

HE HAD ON HIS BRITISH DESIGN HELMET (THE BEST AND SAFEST) and his Davis lamp. Like always, he stepped into the cage first, before the others, all of them: Oren, Dicey, Connie, The Buds (Little Bud and Hey Bud), Hezzie, Luka, a team of 26 men.

No matter how many years they'd been in the mines, the other fellows knew that moment's hesitation, that instant of fear when you understand it is possible for the blackness to engulf you forever.

Buckeye Jim knew darkness. *I was summoned forth from the darkness.*

Don't fear, don't fear. That is what he wanted to tell them, what he wanted to tell everyone. Love one another and do not be afraid.

But they were not ready to hear it yet.

So he smiled the smile that made the others think him a "nice fella," though "no winner in the Mental Olympics, if y'know what I mean." Not that you had to be a chess champion to heft a shovel in a coal mine, and he certainly was one for that!

Buckeye Jim liked the work. He liked the feeling of using his muscles, his back, arms, and legs. He liked the idea that darkness, the coal, became heat and flame.

There was much for Buckeye Jim to like these days. He lived in Spartacus House, one of two company owned residences for single men. It was a lot like an Army barracks, clean, fresh sheets every week, showers with limitless hot water, and detective and science magazines, and a Victrola and a player piano, and pretty pictures on the walls; he paid two dollars a month room and board. He liked the men he lived and worked with. Tonight, he'd go on out with them and have him a beer or two.

And of course he liked to play the banjo—

... ONE HELL OF A PICKER! CARRYING HIS THOMPSON SUB-machine-gun, Charlie Birger walked over to the table of Ft. Lorraine miners at his road-house, The Shady Rest. After 11, but the joint still had a good crowd, even though tomorrow was work day. White and colored drank at the Shady Rest— and if somebody purple showed and had a nickel for a beer, he'd be welcome, too—and there was even a gigantic Ojibway Indian, Big Tommy Tabeshaw, and so at the place, you might hear Italian, Polish, Lithuanian, Rumanian or Ojibway. (When he was really lost in the firewater, Tommy talked to himself and to the "Ojibway ghosts" in his head.)

Charlie told the banjo player that he plainly admired the way he could fram away on that five string.

The banjo player said he appreciated the compliment, but hoped Shady Rest's owner wouldn't get to framming away on his instrument.

Charlie Birger laughed like hell. No, no, no, his Tommy meant protection for himself and his guests. There were some shit heels, Kluxer bastards mostly, didn't like his catering to a "mixed clientele." And, for that matter, they weren't too delighted with Mr. C. Birger, Esquire's, being a co-religionist of Moses.

"My name is Buckeye Jim." The banjo player offered his hand.

He said, "Shalom Aleichem," the traditional Hebrew greeting, "Peace be unto you."

Charlie Birger blanched. "Aleichem Shalom," he said softly. "And unto you, peace."

The gleam in his eyes might have been tears. "You're …"

Buckeye Jim shrugged. "*Vuden?*" Loosely translated, the Yiddish term meant, "What did you expect?"

"I'll be damned," Charlie Birger said. "A hillbilly Yid! A Yid-billy! Well, me, too, I reckon!"

Birger bellowed to the bar, "This gentleman and his friends drink free! Tonight and every night."

He turned back to Buckeye Jim. "You have yourself a friend in Charlie Birger."

"Thank you," Buckeye Jim said. "A man needs all the friends he can get."

Sunday, September 12, 1925

God forgive me, Opal Rae Brown thought. If He did, it would be long before she forgave herself.

Opal Rae puttered about, a huge woman who seemed to fill up all the space in the vast kitchen that had so long been her domain. Oh, Lord, he was a good man and she had to…

He was a white man, she tried to tell herself, and if every white man in the country America decided to swallow a Mason jar full of iodine, lye, and turpentine, now wasn't that just too bad? Besides…

Besides, she was scared, she was scared in every one of her 280 pounds. That man, that Mr. Dupont, had never raised his voice as he told her this, and told her that, as he asked her this and then asked her, "You ever smell black skin burning? You are sort of heavy-set, so I imagine it would take a long time for the fire to bubble and blister and cook all the meat right off your bones."

He gave her orders and the "secret potion" she was to add to the food (Now don't you worry, just some fish eggs and stuff) and 100 dollars. The money would take her north, she vowed. Nobody burned colored people in New York, not as she had heard, anyway.

She took a deep breath, then another.

Then she took Mr. C. Cooper Legrand, Jr. his evening meal. The next day, he was in Ft. Lorraine's hospital, condition—critical.

BUCKEYE JIM COULDN'T SLEEP. HE WENT FOR A WALK, moonlight his guide. At midnight, that empty moment that is neither one day or another, he was far from Ft. Lorraine, deep into the rolling woods. He relished the coolness and earth smells, the myriad night sounds, the eternal celebration and affirmation of life.

Oh, he did not want to die. Not again.

Ahead, on the path that wasn't a path but simply the way he chose, he saw the gleaming eyes. The rattler's precise, gorgeous diamond patterns shone hypnotically. It rose up like a cobra, shifting left and right, the forked tongue a flicker-blur.

Surprised?

"Not hardly," Buckeye Jim said. "Sure you're here. You're everywhere." He took out the lucky buckeye and flipped it, caught it, flipped it. "But you're not going to win, you know. Each time, we get closer."

Fool!

"Fool? Maybe.

"But God needs His fools."

Do you not see? Each time and every time Man is given a chance to damn himself, he says, "Yes, thanks, and might you have a few extra opportunities for my friends?" The victory will be mine!

"No," Buckeye Jim said, "Man is not born to lose." The buckeye flew up high and then higher and came down in his palm. Buckeye Jim grinned.

"Man is born to win."

ON WEDNESDAY, CONDITION NOW "SERIOUS/GUARDED," Legrand had visitors, representatives of the Illinois Coal and Power Company—Mark E. Dupont among them. They did not want to tire him out, to do anything that might slow his recovery.

Inside of 15 minutes, C. Cooper Legrand sold them everything.

VII

Buckeye Jim, weave and spin,
Time to go, Buckeye Jim.
"Buckeye Jim," American folk song

There will always be questions, but I knew C. Cooper Legrand, Jr. I drank coffee with him, went to New York with him to hear Emma Goldman, and spent a long, memorable, mentally exhilarating night, arguing with him over the Nihilistic philosophy of Bakunin; both of us agreed that the man had to be an idiot if all he would allow to go undestroyed would be Beethoven's Sixth, the closest the composer ever came to failure.

Juney Legrand was all right.

So to my dying day, I will not accept that he willfully betrayed the people of Ft. Lorraine or his dream of a world of brotherhood and harmony.

They did something to him. I know they did. As incredible as this may sound, coming from a man who is reputed to be sane, if surly, I have come to believe there are conspiracies meant to stifle and suppress Mankind as we struggle to attain the next step on the moral and ethical evolutionary ladder.

A conspiracy of ???

The Left will tell you it is a wicked collusion of Capital and Government. Too imaginative pulp magazine fans will offer you theories based on a wicked cabal inside our hollow Earth. Then there are preachers who will tell you it is all the work of the Devil...

Brian Robert Moore, "I'll Tell You What!"

Monday, September 27, 1925

IN THE BASEMENT OF FT. LORRAINE'S MASONIC TEMPLE, THEY argued and argued, called each other names, threw about the words, "scab," "fink," and, a phrase frequently used in the American labor movement: "Dumb son of a bitch!" They would march on the state capitol! The nation's capitol! A splinter group said there was a case for assassination—if they could figure out who to assassinate.

They waited to hear from the president of United Mine Workers of America, John L. Lewis. Last time, he said the wrong thing; it provided impetus for the Herrin Massacre of '22.

This time he said nothing.

The Illinois Coal and Power Company meant to take possession of the mines—the town. But damn all and double-damn, it was not the property of I C and P; Ft. Lorraine was their town! The mines were their mines. It was their labor that gave them ownership, their muscle and sweat and not a capitalist's dollars!

It was theirs, damn all!

They meant to keep it!

If it took guns to …

It went on and on, until, at last—

Now they are ready to listen, Buckeye Jim said to himself. He was sad. He liked these men. He did not want to leave them. He thought about bitter cups. He thought about the Lord's will. He thought about what he had to do.

Then Buckeye Jim said he wanted to talk. He talked easy and slow, flipping a buckeye.

He talked and they heard him.

Funny, how a guy you don't figure all that equipped with smartness can talk to you in a way that makes you say, "Why, yes indeed! That is what we have to do."

That is what they did.

They barricaded the northern approach to Ft. Lorraine. They left their guns at home, but they turned over worn-out tin-can cars, piled up bales of hay, and strung barbed wire the way some had learned in the War to End All Wars.

Behind their barricade, they linked arms, the black men and the white men.

They were a living chain across the Washauconda Bridge.

They were ready.

To assist in the I C and P's taking possession of its properties were men in smart-looking uniforms, all duly deputized, bayonets on their rifles.

From Sesser and Marion and Ina and dozens of other towns came non-union miners, needing work, armed with baseball bats, shotguns, pistols, and pitchforks, determined to get these sorry niggers and Bolsheviks out of their way.

Mark E. Dupont led the largest delegation, the stalwarts of the Klan. The Grand Exalted Cyclops, in his robes of flowing white, a regulation Army Springfield under his arm. Now he'd claim...his!

His, damn all! Mr. Mark E. Dupont, the new General Superintendent of I C P's Ft. Lorraine holdings, had the might and purity and right of the Klan stepping smartly behind him, armed with everything from a Quackenbush boy's model single shot to a log chain

The forces of the Illinois Coal and Power Company tramped onward.

The men of Ft. Lorraine waited.

The army of the Illinois Coal and Power Company came closer, ranks tightening as they trod upon the vast length of the Washauconda Bridge.

Waiting them, someone called out, "Stand firm! Union men, comrades in the war!"

Men with bayonets, men in miner's hats, men in KKK garb, moved forward.

The men at the barricades sang:

> *Hold the fort,*
> *Brave union miners!*
> *Show no fear,*
> *Be strong!*

At the other end of the bridge, taunting voices called, "Let's kill us some niggers!"

"Turkey shoot! They ain't got a gobbler's chance!"

The I C and P troops drew closer. The bridge shook with their out-of-step march. The collage of sounds was sinister and portentous: muttering and shouts, the hiss and whisper and bubblings of the Washauconda below, the click-ready sound of firearms.

You could smell oil and gunpowder.

"You are an unlawful assembly, blocking a public thoroughfare!" Dupont called out. "Give way immediately or perish!" He liked the formality of his proclamation.

He did not like the roared response it drew from a defender of Ft. Lorraine: "You get up on your momma's shoulders and kiss my ass."

When less than a hundred yards separated the men of Ft. Lorraine from the I C and P forces, Buckeye Jim suddenly appeared between them.

Quizzical, because nobody really saw him walk there, but there he was.

It stopped them all.

Buckeye Jim wasn't flipping a lucky buckeye. Not this time. He had his arms up and out, as though he were Moses helping God, pushing back the walls of water to part the Red Sea. There are some still living who, even to this very day, will tell you the man was transfigured.

Buckeye Jim had something to say.

NOTHING HAPPENED HE DIDN'T KNOW ABOUT. NOT IN HIS kingdom.

Because—you'd better know it and you're mighty well told!—Charlie Birger was the King of Egypt!

Ft. Lorraine? Good boys, there, and his Yid friend, Buckeye Jim, so…

Time for damned sure to hitch the horses to the king's chariot.

Except he didn't need horses.

Everyone stayed quiet. Everyone heard him.

He said, "Some of you don't know me, and some of you know me as Buckeye Jim. But years back, years and years and years ago, I was the one they talk about in the Bible. They call me 'The Widow's Son.' I was dead, just as dead as Mr. Lazarus, but then Jesus called to me and said, 'Come forth from your tomb.'

"Well, I was grateful and such, and I politely thanked Him, but I asked him why He had summoned me from the ever-dark of death into the light of life.

"Didn't I like being alive? Didn't I want to do the work of the living God, the God of the living?

"I thought about that and thought about that—

"Until I said, 'Why, yes, I guess I do.'

"Now this is what Jesus told me. This is what He wants me to tell you.

"Jesus came to bring hope. He said it was my job to be hope, because I'd been dead and now I was alive.

"We are all the children of God. The Devil and the darkness will never defeat us!

"Jesus told me something more.

"He said He would come again.

"He said He would return—on the day after He no longer was needed!

"That means it's up to us to set it all right.

"And we can start to do that. We can start now."

There was silence.

And almost everyone stood frozen.

But not Mark E. Dupont, who thought, The Devil can quote scripture for his own purpose. Dupont slammed the stock of his Springfield into his shoulder and fired.

The bullet caught Buckeye Jim just to the left of the heart. He flew backward, slammed into the bridge railing a slice of an instant after his blood and fragments of bone did, and, loose limbed, flipped over. If his body splashed as it plunged into the river, no one heard it.

The I C and P forces let out a collective yell that drowned out a sudden roar of thunder in the clear sky above.

They charged.

"GIVE IT ALL YOU'VE GOT," CHARLIE BIRGER COMMANDED. The driver of the brand new armored car obliged. The powerful Stutz engine thrummed. The heavy sheet metal riveted and welded to the auto slowed it and guaranteed nothing could stand in its way. Instead of a windshield or windows, the car had gun slits. Except for treads, it was a tank—and its solid rubber tires weren't about to be knocked out by any varmint hunter's firepower.

It was the lead vehicle of three. Two cars loaded with Birger men followed

Charlie might have been confused, once they hit the bridge, but the KKK bastards, decked out like Monday wash on the line, why he knew who to shoot! So Charlie popped the heavy hatch, and rose up to let loose with a quick spray from Mr. Tommy. One blast felt so fine, the gun a roaring quiver in his hands, that he fired off another. He heard the guns of his army behind him. He saw the befuddled I C P men turn, trying to figure what the hell. There was sporadic return fire, slugs pinging off the metal around him.

"Welcome to Egypt's O.K. Corral," Charlie yelled. He laughed and fired off another burst.

Then another.

With the next one, he totally hem-stitched Mark E. Dupont.

Inside of three minutes, 43 men lay dead on the Washauconda bridge, most of them Kluxers; another 75 or 81 or 58 (depending on which account of the conflict you believe) were wounded and conveyed to area hospitals.

Most historians cite the "Battle of Washauconda Bridge" as the end of the Klan's power in southern Illinois.

Charlie Birger and his warriors retreated to Shady Rest and drank beer. The King could not figure where Buckeye Jim might have disappeared to. He hoped he would turn up. He wished him luck.

Fellow played one fine banjo.

EPILOGUE

M ark E. Dupont received one of the most elaborate Klan funerals in the history of the organization. A vice-president of I C and P gave the eulogy, saying Dupont was one of the company's finest assistant superintendents; after the funeral, he presented Mrs. Dupont with a check for 50 dollars.

Virtually everyone employed by the Old Legrand and Washauconda River Mining Corporation was fired and had to leave Ft. Lorraine. The union did not regain any foothold in the region until FDR.

Charlie Birger had a falling out with Joe Adams, who'd built "The King of Egypt's" armored car, and was convicted of arranging the man's murder.

Charlie was hanged on April 18, 1929, the last man legally executed in this way in the state. Legend has it that the night before his execution, Charlie had a lanky visitor, who talked and joked a while with him, then handed him a buckeye.

Perhaps that is the reason that, on the scaffold, Charlie's last words were, "It is a beautiful world.

"Goodbye."

stay quiet.
"Some of you don't know

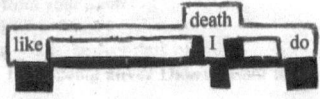

like death I do

this is

my job to be

the children of

bullet

a bone
rive n ead
roar of thunder in

all
The

to

follow

The Night Wire

The darkness
The sickly ash
The unusual fog in the churchyard.
It was not a curse from the grave.
It was a rescue party.

THE NIGHT WIRE

BY H. F. ARNOLD

The first time I read "The Night Wire" by H. F. Arnold, I was determined to find more of his work. He had to have an obscure, little known collection full of amazing stories, right? Much to my surprise, not only was there no collection and only two other stories (which, to this day, I still haven't read), but also — no one really knows who H. F. Arnold was. There's a few guesses in regards to men with similar initials (one of the most referenced candidates is Henry Ferris Arnold, a press agent who worked in Hollywood, but I'm not sure if that was ever confirmed), but to this day, I don't think anyone really knows who he was. I could be wrong, of course, and welcome the confirmation!

Or...maybe I don't. Maybe I prefer the mystery. It seems fitting that an unknown man would write a story full of

*creeping dread and cosmic horror about an unknown town
no one can find on a map, anywhere..*

New York, September 30 CP FLASH

*"Ambassador Holliwell died here today.
The end came suddenly as the ambassador was
alone in his study...."*

There's something ungodly about these night wire jobs. You sit up here on the top floor of a skyscraper and listen in to the whispers of a civilization. New York, London, Calcutta, Bombay, Singapore—they're your next-door neighbors after the street lights go dim and the world has gone to sleep.

Along in the quiet hours between 2 and 4, the receiving operators doze over their sounders and the news comes in. Fires and disasters and suicides. Murders, crowds, catastrophes. Sometimes an earthquake with a casualty list as long as your arm. The night wire man takes it down almost in his sleep, picking it off on his typewriter with one finger.

Once in a long time you prick up your ears and listen. You've heard of someone you knew in Singapore, Halifax or Paris, long ago. Maybe they've been promoted, but more probably they've been murdered or drowned. Perhaps they just decided to quit and took some bizarre way out. Made it interesting enough to get in the news.But that doesn't happen often. Most of the time you sit and doze and tap, tap on your typewriter and wish you were home in bed.

Sometimes, though, queer things happen. One did the other night and I haven't got over it yet. I wish I could.

You see, I handle the night manager's desk in a western seaport town; what the name is, doesn't matter. There is, or rather was, only one night operator on my staff, a fellow named John Morgan, about forty years of age, I should say, and a sober, hard-working sort.

He was one of the best operators I ever knew, what is known as a "double" man. That means he could handle two instruments at once and type the stories on different typewriters at the same time. He was one of the three men I ever knew who could do it consistently, hour after hour, and never make a mistake.

Generally we used only one wire at night, but sometimes, when it was late and the news was coming fast, the Chicago and Denver stations would open a second wire and then Morgan would do his stuff. He was a wizard, a mechanical automatic wizard which functioned marvelously but was without imagination.

On the night of the sixteenth he complained of feeling tired. It was the first and last time I had ever heard him say a word about himself, and I had known him for three years.

It was at just 3 o'clock and we were running only one wire. I was nodding over reports at my desk and not paying much attention to him when he spoke.

"Jim," he said, "does it feel close in here to you?"

"Why, no, John," I answered, "but I'll open a window if you like."

"Never mind," he said. "I reckon I'm just a little tired."

That was all that was said and I went on working. Every ten minutes or so I would walk over and take a pile of copy that had stacked up neatly beside his typewriter as the messages were printed out in triplicate.

It must have been twenty minutes after he spoke that I noticed he had opened up the other wire and was using both typewriters. I thought it was a little unusual, as there was nothing very "hot" coming in. On my next trip I picked up the copy from both machines and took it back to my desk to sort out the duplicates.

The first wire was running out the usual sort of stuff and I just looked over it hurriedly. Then I turned to the second pile of copy. I remember it particularly because the story was from a town I had never heard of: "Xebico." Here is the dispatch. I saved a duplicate of it from our files:

Xebico Sept. 16 CP BULLETIN

"The heaviest mist in the history of the city settled over the town at 4 o'clock yesterday afternoon. All traffic has stopped and the mist hangs like a pall over everything. Lights of ordinary intensity fail to pierce the fog, which is constantly growing heavier.

"Scientists here are unable to agree as to the cause, and the local weather bureau states that the like has never occurred before in the history of the city.

"At 7 p. m. last night municipal authorities (more)"

That was all there was. Nothing out of the ordinary at a bureau headquarters, but, as I say, I noticed the story because of the name of the town.

It must have been fifteen minutes later that I went over for another batch of copy. Morgan was slumped down in his chair and had switched his green electric light shade so that the gleam missed his eyes and hit only the top of the two typewriters.

Only the usual stuff was in the right hand pile, but the left hand batch carried another story from "Xebico." All press dispatches come in "takes," meaning that parts of many different stories are strung along together, perhaps with but a few paragraphs of each coming through at a time. This second story was marked "add fog." Here is the copy:

"At 7 p. m. the fog had increased noticeably. All lights were now invisible and the town was shrouded in pitch darkness.

"As a peculiarity of the phenomenon, the fog is accompanied by a sickly odor, comparable to nothing yet experienced here."

Below that in customary press fashion was the hour, 3:27, and the initials of the operator, JM.

There was only one other story in the pile from the second wire. Here it is:

2nd add Xebico Fog

"Accounts as to the origin of the mist differ greatly. Among the most unusual is that of the sexton of the local church, who groped his way to headquarters in a hysterical condition and declared that the fog originated in the village churchyard." 'It was first visible in the shape of a soft gray blanket clinging to the earth above the graves,' he stated. 'Then it began to rise, higher and higher. A subterranean breeze seemed to blow it in billows, which split up and then joined together again.' "Fog phantoms, writhing in anguish, twisted the mist into queer forms and figures. And then—in the very thick midst of the mass—something moved.

" 'I turned and ran from the accursed spot. Behind me I heard screams coming from the houses bordering on the graveyard.'

"Although the sexton's story is generally discredited, a party has left to investigate. Immediately after telling his story, the sexton collapsed and is now in a local hospital, unconscious."

Queer story, wasn't it? Not that we aren't used to it, for a lot of unusual stories come in over the wire. But for some reason or other, perhaps because it was so quiet that night, the report of the fog made a great impression on me.

It was almost with dread that I went over to the waiting piles of copy. Morgan did not move and the only sound in the room was the tap-tap of the sounders. It was ominous, nerve-racking.

There was another story from Xebico in the pile of copy. I seized on it anxiously

New Lead Xebico Fog CP

"The rescue party which went out at 11 p. m. to investigate a weird story of the origin of a fog which, since late yesterday, has shrouded the city in darkness, has failed to return. Another and larger party has been dispatched.

"Meanwhile the fog has, if possible, grown heavier. It seeps through the cracks in the doors and fills the atmosphere with a terribly depressing odor of decay. It is oppressive, terrifying, bearing with it a subtle impression of things long dead.

"Residents of the city have left their homes and gathered in the local church, where the priests are holding services of prayer. The scene is beyond description. Grown folk and children are alike terrified and many are almost beside themselves with fear.

"Mid the wisps of vapor which partially veil the church auditorium, an old priest is praying for the welfare of his flock. The audience alternately wail and cross themselves.

"From the outskirts of the city may be heard cries of unknown voices. They echo through the fog in queer uncadenced minor keys. The

sounds resemble nothing so much as wind whis-
tling through a gigantic tunnel. But the night is
calm and there is no wind. The second rescue
party—(more)"

I am a calm man and never in a dozen years spent with the wires have been known to become excited, but despite myself I rose from my chair and walked to the window.

Could I be mistaken, or far down in the canyons of the city beneath me did I see a faint trace of fog? Pshaw! It was all imagination.

In the pressroom the click of the sounders seemed to have raised the tempo of their tune. Morgan alone had not stirred from his chair. His head sunk between his shoulders, he tapped the dispatches out on the typewriters with one finger of each hand.

He looked asleep. Maybe he was—but no, endlessly, efficiently, the two machines rattled off line after line, as relentless and effortless as death itself. There was something about the monotonous movement of the typewriter keys that fascinated me. I walked over and stood behind his chair reading over his shoulder the type as it came into being, word by word.

Ah, here was another:

Flash Xebico CP

"There will be no more bulletins from this
office. The impossible has happened. No mes-
sages have come into this room for twenty min-
utes. We are cut off from the outside and even
the streets below us.

"I will stay with the wire until the end.

"It is the end, indeed. Since 4 p. m. yesterday
the fog has hung over the city. Following reports
from the sexton of the local church, two rescue

parties were sent out to investigate conditions on the outskirts of the city. Neither party has ever returned nor was any word received from them. It is quite certain now that they will never return.

"From my instrument I can gaze down on the city beneath me. From the position of this room on the thirteenth floor, nearly the entire city can be seen. Now I can see only a thick blanket of blackness where customarily are lights and life.

"I fear greatly that the wailing cries heard constantly from the outskirts of the city are the death cries of the inhabitants. They are constantly increasing in volume and are approaching the center of the city.

"The fog yet hangs over everything. If possible, it is even heavier than before. But the conditions have changed. Instead of an opaque, impenetrable wall of odorous vapor, now swirls and writhes a shapeless mass in contortions of almost human agony. Now and again the mass parts and I catch a brief glimpse of the streets below.

"People are running to and fro, screaming in despair. A vast bedlam of sound flies up to my window, and above all is the immense whistling of unseen and unfelt winds.

"The fog has again swept over the city and the whistling is coming closer and closer.

"It is now directly beneath me.

"God! An instant ago the mist opened and I caught a glimpse of the streets below.

"The fog is not simply vapor—it lives. By the side of each moaning and weeping human is a companion figure, an aura of strange and vari-colored hues. How the shapes cling! Each to a living thing!

"The men and women are down. Flat on their faces. The fog figures caress them lovingly.

They are kneeling beside them. They are—but I dare not tell it.

"The prone and writhing bodies have been stripped of their clothing. They are being consumed—piecemeal.

"A merciful wall of hot, steamy vapor has swept over the whole scene. I can see no more.

"Beneath me the wall of vapor is changing colors. It seems to be lighted by internal fires. No, it isn't. I have made a mistake. The colors are from above, reflections from the sky.

"Look up! Look up! The whole sky is in flames. Colors as yet unseen by man or demon. The flames are moving, they have started to intermix, the colors rearrange themselves. They are so brilliant that my eyes burn, yet they are a long way off.

"Now they have begun to swirl, to circle in and out, twisting in intricate designs and patterns. The lights are racing each with each, a kaleidoscope of unearthly brilliance.

"I have made a discovery. There is nothing harmful in the lights. They radiate force and friendliness, almost cheeriness. But by their very strength, they hurt.

"As I look they are swinging closer and closer, a million miles at each jump. Millions of miles with the speed of light. Aye, it is light, the quintessence of all light. Beneath it the fog melts into a jeweled mist, radiant, rainbow-colored of a thousand varied spectrums.

"I can see the streets. Why, they are filled with people! The lights are coming closer. They are all around me. I am enveloped. I——"

The message stopped abruptly. The wire to Xebico was dead. Beneath my eyes in the narrow circle of light from under the green lampshade, the black printing no longer spun itself, letter by letter, across the page.

The room seemed filled with a solemn quiet, a silence vaguely impressive. Powerful.

I looked down at Morgan. His hands had dropped nervelessly at his sides while his body had hunched over peculiarly. I turned the lampshade back, throwing the light squarely in his face. His eyes were staring, fixed. Filled with a sudden foreboding, I stepped beside him and called Chicago on the wire. After a second the sounder clicked its answer.

Why? But there was something wrong. Chicago was reporting that Wire Two had not been used throughout the evening.

"Morgan!" I shouted. "Morgan! Wake up, it isn't true. Someone has been hoaxing us. Why——" In my eagerness I grasped him by the shoulder. It was only then that I understood.

The body was quite cold. Morgan had been dead for hours. Could it be that his sensitized brain and automatic fingers had continued to record impressions even after the end?

I shall never know, for I shall never again handle the night shift. Search in a world atlas discloses no town of Xebico. Whatever it was that killed John Morgan will forever remain a mystery.

"At 7 p. m. the fog had increased noticeably. All lights were now invisible and the town was shrouded in pitch darkness.

.As a peculiarity of the phenomenon the fog is accompanied by sickly odor, comparable to nothing yet experienced here..

Below that in customary press flash was the hour, 3:27, and the initials of the operator, JM. There was only one other story in the pile from the second wire. Here it is:

2nd add Xebico Fog

Accounts as to the origin of the mist differ greatly. Among the unusual the sexton of the local church, who groped his way to headquarters physical condition and declared that the fog originated in the village churchyard. 'It was first visible in the shape of a soft gray th above the graves,' he stated. Then it began to rise, higher and higher seemed to blow it in pillows, which split up and then .'Fog phantoms, writhing in anguish mist into forms and figures. And then.in the very thick midst of the .'I turned and ran from the curse coming from the houses bordering on the graveyard.

.Although the discreetly has to investigate. Immediately after telling his story collapsed and local hospital unconscious..

Queer story, wasn't it? Not that we aren't used to it, for a lot of unusual stories come in over the wire. But for some reason or things because it was so quiet that night, the report of the fog made **a great impression on me.** It was almost with dread that I went over to the working piles of copy. Morgan did not move and the in the room was the tap-tap of the sounders. It was ominous, nerve-racking. There was another story from Xebico in the pile of copy. I seized on it anxiously

New Lead Xebico Fog CF

rescue party which to investigate word story of the origin of a fog the city in has failed to return. Another and ryer party has been

Meanwhile the fog grows heavier through the cracks in the doors and the atmosphere depressing odor is oppressive, terrifying, bearing with it a subtle long dead. .Residents their homes and the local church, where the priests are holding the scene is beyond Grown folk and children are alike beside themselves with Within the partially veil the torium, an old priest is praying for audience alternately and themselves. of the city may be heard nown voices. They echo through the minor keys. The nothing so much as wind whistling el. But the night is is no wind. The second rescue party.

The Night We Bried Road Dog

From the grave, new grass sprouted.
Wildflowers climbed.
Birds called from high places.

I wished for a lot of things.
Love,
Magic,
The dancing ghost of midnight.
When he was around, I found it.
I bloomed.
When my best friend, The Dog, was chasing me.

But the extra-special comes with flowers that die
As I try to go on
Chasing The Dog.

THE NIGHT WE BURIED ROAD DOG

BY JACK CADY

It's hard to put into words how I feel about this story, because it's one of the very first I read that made me realize how much of horror's history stands threatened to be lost to the sands of time. It was in a Cemetery Dance collection called, **Stoker Hall of Fame,** *collecting works which had Stoker Awards over the years. I was still a young horror writer, and — to my shame — I think the first few pages I get a little "bored," wondering where the "horror" was.*

As I kept reading, however, a ghostly sense of foreboding had wormed its way into my heart, and I was hooked. And then when I realized what the story's true "horror" was, I turned a corner in my mind, knowing that as a reader and writer of horror, I'd never be the same again.

I

Brother Jesse buried his '47 Hudson back in '61 and the roads got just that much more lonesome. Highway 2 across north Montana still wailed with engines as reservation cars blew past; and it lay like a tunnel of darkness before headlights of big rigs. Tandems pounded, and the smart crack of downshifts rapped across grassland as trucks swept past the bars at every crossroad. The state put up metal crosses to mark the sites of fatal accidents. Around the bars those crosses sprouted like thickets.

That Hudson was named Miss Molly, and it logged two hundred twenty thousand miles while never burning a clutch. Through the years it wore into the respectable look that comes to old machinery. It was rough as a cob, cracked glass on one side, and primer over dents. It had the tough and ready look of a hunting hound about its business. I was a good deal younger then, but not so young that I was fearless.

The burial had something to do with mystery, and brother Jesse did his burying at midnight.

Through fluke or foresight, brother Jesse had got hold of eighty acres of rangeland that wasn't worth a shake. There wasn't enough of it to run stock, and you couldn't raise anything on it except a little hell. Jesse stuck an old housetrailer out there, stacked hay around it for insulation in Montana winters, and hauled in just enough water to suit him. By the time his Hudson died he was ready to go into trade.

"Jed," he told me the night of the burial, "I'm gonna make myself some history, despite this damn Democrat administration." Over beside the housetrailer the Hudson sat looking like it was about ready to get off the mark in a road race, but the poor thing was a goner. Moonlight sprang from between spring clouds, and to the westward the peaks of mountains glowed from snow and moonlight. Along highway 2 some hotrock wound second gear on an old flathead Ford. You could hear the valves begin to float.

"Some little darlin' done stepped on that boy's balls," Jesse said about the driver. "I reckon that's why he's looking for a ditch." Jesse sighed and sounded sad. "At least we got a nice night. I couldn't stand a winter funeral."

"Road Dog?" I said about the driver of the Ford, which shows just how young I was at the time.

"It ain't The Dog," Jesse told me. "The Dog's a damn survivor."

YOU NEVER KNEW WHERE BROTHER JESSE GOT HIS STUFF, AND you never really knew if he was anybody's brother. The only time I asked, he said, "I come from a close knit family such as your own," and that made no sense. My own father died when I was twelve, and my mother married again when I turned seventeen. She picked up and moved to Wisconsin.

No one even knew when, or how, Jesse got to Montana territory. We just looked up one day and there he was as natural as if he'd always been here, and maybe he always had.

His eighty acres began to fill up. Old printing presses stood gap-mouthed like spinsters holding conversation. A salvaged greenhouse served for storing dog food, engine parts, chromium hair dryers from 1930's-beauty-shops, dimestore pottery, blades for hay cutters, binder twine, an old gas-powered cross-cut saw, seats from a schoolbus, and a bunch of other stuff not near as useful.

A couple of tabbies lived in that greenhouse, but the Big Cat stood outside. It was an old D6 bulldozer with a shovel, and Jesse stoked it up from time to time. Mostly, it just sat there. In summers it provided shade for Jesse's dogs: Potato was brown and fat and not too bright, while Chip was little and fuzzy. Sometimes they rode with Jesse, and sometimes stayed home. Me or Mike Tarbush fed them. When anything big happened you could count on those two dogs to get underfoot. Except for me, they were the only ones who attended the funeral.

"If we gotta do it," Jesse said mournfully, "we gotta." He wound up the Cat, turned on the headlights, and headed for the gravesite which was an embankment overlooking highway 2. Back in those days Jesse's hair still shone black, and it was even blacker in the darkness. It dangled around a face that carried an Indian forehead and a Scotsman's nose. Denim stretched across most of the six feet of him, and he wasn't rangy, he was thin. He had feet to match his height, and his hands seemed bigger than his feet; but the man could skin a Cat.

I stood in moonlight and watched him work. A little puff of flame dwelt in the stack of the bulldozer. It flashed against the darkness of those distant mountains. It burbled hot in the cold spring moonlight. Jesse made rough cuts pretty quick, moved a lot of soil, then started getting delicate. He shaped and reshaped that grave. He carved a little from one side, backed the dozer, found his cut not satisfactory. He took a spoonful of earth to straighten things, then fussed with the grade leading into the grave. You could tell he wanted a slight elevation, so the Hudson's nose would be sniffing toward the road. Old Potato-dog had a hound's ears, but not a hound's good sense. He started baying at the moon.

It came to me that I was scared. Then it came to me that I was scared most of the time, anyway. I was nineteen, and folks talked about having a war across the sea. I didn't want to hear about it. On top of the war talk, women were driving me crazy; the ones who said 'no' and the ones who said 'yes.' It got downright mystifying just trying to figure out which was worse. At nineteen it's hard to know how to act. There were whole weeks when I could pass myself off as a hellion, then something would go sour. I'd get hit by a streak of conscience and start acting like a missionary.

"Jed," Jesse told me from the seat of the dozer, "go rig a tow on Miss Molly." In the headlights, the grave now looked like a garage dug into the side of that little slope. Brother Jesse eased the Cat back in there to fuss with the grade. I stepped slow toward the Hudson, wiggled under, and fetched the towing cable around the frame. Potato howled. Chip danced like a fuzzy fury, and started chewing on my boot like he's trying to drag me from under the Hudson. I'm on my back trying to kick Chip away and secure the cable. Then I like to died from fright.

Nothing else in the world sounds anywhere near like a Hudson starter. It's a combination of whine and clatter and growl. If I'd been dead a thousand years you could stand me right up with a Hudson starter. There's threat in that sound. There's also the promise that things can get pretty rowdy, pretty quick.

The starter went off. The Hudson jiggled. In the one-half second it took to get from under that car I thought of every bad thing I ever did in my life. I was headed for hell, certain sure. By the time I was on my feet there wasn't an ounce of blood showing anywhere on me. When the old folks say, 'white as a sheet,' they're talking about a guy under a Hudson.

Brother Jesse climbed from the Cat and gave me a couple of shakes.

"She ain't dead," I stuttered. "The engine turned over. Miss Molly's still thinking speedy." From highway 2 came the wail of Mike Tarbush's '48 Roadmaster. Mike loved and cussed that car. It always flattened out at around eighty.

"There's still some sap left in the batt'ry," Jesse said about the Hudson. "You probably caused a short." He dropped the cable around the hitch on the dozer. "Steer her," he said.

The steering wheel still felt alive, despite what Jesse said. I crouched behind the wheel as the Hudson got dragged toward the grave. Its brakes locked twice, but the towing cable held. The locked brakes caused the car to side-slip. Each time Jesse cussed. Cold spring moonlight made the shadowed grave look like a cave of darkness.

The Hudson bided its time. We got it lined up, then pushed it backwards into the grave. The hunched front fenders spread beside the snarly grill. The front bumper was the only thing about that car that still showed clean and uncluttered. I could swear Miss Molly moved in the darkness of the grave, about to come charging onto highway 2. Then she seemed to make some kind of decision, and sort of settled down. Jesse gave the eulogy.

"This here car never did nothing bad," he said. "I must have seen a million crap-crates, but this car wasn't one of them. She had a second gear like hydramatic, and you could wind to 70 before you dropped to third. There wasn't no top end to her, at least I never had the guts to find it. This here was a 100 mile-an-hour car on a bad night, and God-knows-what on a good'n."

From highway 2 you could hear the purr of Matt Simon's '56 Dodge, five speeds, what with the overdrive, and Matt was scorching.

Potato howled long and mournful. Chip whined. Jesse scratched his head, trying to figure a way to end the eulogy. It came to him like a blessing. "I can't prove it," he said, "'cause no one could. But, I expect this car has passed The Road Dog maybe a couple of hundred times." He made like he was going to cross himself, then remembered he was Methodist. "Rest in peace," he said, and he said it with eyes full of tears. "There ain't that many who can comprehend The Dog." He climbed back on the Cat and began to fill the grave.

Next day Jesse mounded the grave with real care. He erected a marker, although the marker was more like a little signboard:

1947–1961

Hudson coupe—'Molly'

220,023 miles on straight eight cylinder

Died of busted crankshaft

Beloved in the memory of

Jesse Still

MONTANA ROADS ARE LONG AND LONESOME, AND HIGHWAY 2 IS lonesomest. You pick it up over on the Idaho border where the land is mountains. Bear and cougar still live pretty good, and beaver still build dams. The highway runs beside some pretty lakes. Canada is no more than a jump away; it hangs at your left shoulder when you're headed east.

And can you roll those mountains? Yes, oh yes. It's two lane all the way across, and twisty in the hills. From Libby you ride down to Kalispell, then pop back north. The hills last 'til the Blackfoot reservation. It's rangeland into Cut Bank, then to Havre. That's just about the center of the state.

Just let the engine howl from town to town. The road goes through a dozen, then swings south. And there you are at Glasgow and the river. By Wolf Point you're in cropland, and it's flat from there until Chicago.

I almost hate to tell about this road, because Easterners may want to come and visit. Then they'll do something dumb at a blind entry. The state will erect more metal crosses. Enough folks die up here already. And, it's sure no place for rice grinders, or tacky Swedish station wagons, or high priced German crap crates. This was always a V8 road, and V12 if you had 'em. In the old, old days there were even a few V16s up here. The top end on those things came when friction stripped the tires from too much speed.

S<small>PEED OR NOT, BRAKES SURE SOUNDED AS CARS PASSED</small> M<small>ISS</small> Molly's grave. Pickup trucks fishtailed as men snapped them to the shoulder. The men would sit in their trucks for a minute, scratching their heads like they couldn't believe what they'd just seen. Then they'd climb from the truck, walk back to the grave, and read the marker. About half of them would start holding their sides. One guy even rolled around on the ground, he was laughing so much.

"These old boys are laughing now," Brother Jesse told me, "but I predict a change in attitude. I reckon they'll come around before first snowfall."

With his car dead, Jesse had to find a set of wheels. He swapped an old hay rake and a gang of discs for a '49 Chevrolet.

"It wouldn't pull the doorknob off a cathouse," he told me. "It's just to get around in while I shop."

The whole deal was going to take some time. Knowing Jesse, I figured he'd go through half a dozen trades before finding something comfortable. And, I was right.

He first showed up in an old Packard hearse that once belonged to a funeral home in Billings. He'd swapped the Chev for the hearse, plus a gilt-covered coffin so gaudy it wouldn't fit anybody but a radio preacher. He swapped the hearse to Sam Winder, who aimed to use it for hunting trips. Sam's dogs wouldn't go anywhere near the thing. Sam opened all the windows and the back door, then took the hearse up to speed trying to blow out all the ghosts. The dogs still wouldn't go near it. Sam said 'to hell with it' and pushed it into a ravine. Every rabbit and fox and varmint in that ravine came bailing out, and nobody has gone in there ever since.

Jesse traded the coffin to old man Jefferson who parked the thing in his woodshed. Jefferson was supposed to be on his last legs, but figured he wasn't ever, never, going to die if his poor body knew it would be buried in that monstrosity. It worked for several years, too, until a bad winter came along and he split it up for firewood. But, we still remember him.

Jesse came out of those trades with a '47 Pontiac and a Model T. He sold the Model T to a collector, then traded the Pontiac and forty bales of hay for a '53 Studebaker. He swapped the Studebaker for a ratty pickup and all the equipment in a restaurant that went bust. He peddled the equipment to some other poor fellow who was hell-bent to go bust in the restaurant business. Then he traded the pickup for a motorcycle, plus a '51 Plymouth that would just about get out of its own way. By the time he peddled both of them he had his pockets full of cash and was riding shank's mare.

"Jed," he told me, "let's you and me go to the big city." He was pretty happy, but I remembered how scared I'd been at the funeral. I admit to being skittish.

From the center of north Montana there weren't a championship lot of big cities. West was Seattle, which was sort of rainy and mythological. North was Winnipeg, a cow town. South was

Salt Lake City. To the east . . .

"The hell with it," Brother Jesse said, "we'll go to Minneapolis."

It was about a thousand miles. Maybe fifteen hours, what with the roads. You could sail Montana and North Dakota, but those Minnesota cops were humorless.

I was shoving a sweet old '53 Desoto. It had a good bit under the bonnet, but the suspension would make a grown man cry. It was a beautiful beast, though. Once you got up to speed that front end would track like a cat. The upholstery was like brand new. The radio worked. There wasn't a scratch or ding on it. I had myself a banker's car, and there I was, only 19.

"We may want to loiter," Jesse told me. "Plan on a couple of overnights."

I had a job, but told myself that I was due for vacation; and so screw it. Brother Jesse put down food for the tabbies, and whistled up the dogs. Potato hopped into the back seat in his large, dumb way. He looked expectant. Chip sort of hesitated. He made a couple of jumps straight up, then backed down and started barking. Jesse scooped him up and shoved him in with old Potato-dog.

"The upholstery," I hollered. It was the first time I ever stood up to Jesse.

Jesse got an old piece of tarp to put under the dogs. "Pee and you're a goner," he told Potato.

We drove steady through the early summer morning. The Desoto hung in around eighty, which was no more than you'd want considering the suspension. Rangeland gave way to cropland. The radio plugged away with western music, beef prices, and an occasional preacher saying 'grace' and 'gimmie.' Highway 2 rolled straight ahead, sometimes rising gradual, so that cars appeared like rapid running spooks out of the blind entries. There'd be a little flash of sunlight from a windshield. Then a car would appear over the rise, and usually it was wailing.

We came across a hell of a wreck just beyond Havre. A new Mercury station wagon rolled about fifteen times across the landscape. There were two nice-dressed people and two children. Not one of them ever stood a chance. They rattled like dice in a drum. I didn't want to see what I was looking at.

Bad wrecks always made me sick, but not sick to puking. That would not have been manly. I prayed for those people under my breath and got all shaky. We pulled into a crossroads bar for a sandwich and a beer. The dogs hopped out. Plenty of hubcaps were nailed on the wall of the bar. We took a couple of them down, and filled them with water from an outside tap. The dogs drank and peed.

"I've attended a couple myself," Brother Jesse said about the wreck. "Drove a Terraplane off a bridge back in '53. Damn near drowned." Jesse wasn't about to admit to feeling bad. He just turned thoughtful.

"This here is a big territory," he said to no one in particular. "But you can get across her if you hustle. I reckon that Merc was loaded wrong, or blew a tire." Beyond the windows of the bar eight metal crosses lined the highway. Somebody had tied red plastic roses on one of them. Another one had plastic violets and forget-me-nots.

We lingered a little. Jesse talked to the guy at the bar, and I ran a rack at the pool table. Then Jesse bought a six pack while I headed for the can. Since it was still early in the day the can was clean; all the last night's pee and spit mopped from the floor. Somebody had just painted the walls. There wasn't a thing written on them, except that Road Dog had signed in.

> *Road Dog*
> *How are things in Glocca Mora?*

His script was spidery and perfect, like an artist who drew a signature. I touched the paint and it was still tacky. We had missed The Dog by only a few minutes.

ROAD DOG WAS LIKE JESSE IN A WAY. NOBODY COULD SAY exactly when he showed up, but one day he was there. We started seeing the name 'Road Dog' written in what Matt

Simons called 'a fine, Spencerian hand.' There was always a message attached, and Matt called them 'cryptic.' The signature and messages flashed from the walls of cans in bars, truck stops, and roadside cafes through four states.

We didn't know Road Dog's route at first. Most guys were tied to work or home or laziness. In a year or two, though, Road Dog's trail got mapped. His fine hand showed up all along highway 2, trailed east into North Dakota, dropped south through South Dakota, then ran back west across Wyoming. He popped north through Missoula and climbed the state until he connected with highway 2 again. Road Dog, whoever he was, ran a constant square of road that covered roughly two thousand miles.

Sam Winder claimed Road Dog was a communist who taught social studies at U. of Montana. "Because," Sam claimed, "that kind of writing comes from Europe. That writing ain't U.S.A."

Mike Tarbush figured Road Dog was a retired cartoonist from a newspaper. He figured nobody could spot The Dog, because The Dog slipped past us in a Nash, or some other old granny car.

Brother Jesse suggested that Road Dog was a truck driver, or maybe a gypsy, but sounded like he knew better.

Matt Simons supposed Road Dog was a traveling salesman with a flair for advertising. Matt based his notion on one of the cryptic messages:

Road Dog
Ringling Bros. Barnum and Toothpaste

I didn't figure anything. Road Dog stood in my imagination as the heart and soul of highway 2. When night was deep and engines blazed, I could hang over the wheel and run down that tunnel of two lane into the night.

The nighttime road is different than any other thing. Ghosts rise around the metal crosses, and ghosts hitchhike along the wide berm. All the mysteries of the world seem normal after dark. If imagination shows dead thumbs aching for a ride, those dead folk only prove the hot and spermy goodness of life. I'd overtake some taillights, grab the other lane, and blow doors off some partygoer who tried to stay out of the ditches. A man can sing and cuss and pray. The miles fill with dreams of power, and women, and happy, happy times.

Road Dog seemed part of that romance. He was the very soul of mystery; a guy who looked at the dark heart of the road and still flew free enough to make jokes and write that fine hand.

In daytime it was different, though. When I saw Road Dog signed in on the wall of that can, it just seemed like a real bad sign.

THE GUY WHO OWNED THE BAR HAD SEEN NO ONE. HE CLAIMED he'd been in the back room putting bottles in his cold case. The Dog had come and gone like a spirit.

Jesse and I stood in the parking lot outside the bar. Sunlight laid earthy and hot across new crops. A little puff of dust rose from a side road. It advanced real slow, so you could tell it was a farm tractor. All around us, meadowlarks and tanagers were whooping it up.

"We'll likely pass him," Jesse said, "if we crowd a little." Jesse pretended he didn't care, but anyone would. We loaded the dogs, and even hung the hubcaps back up where we got them, because it was what a gentleman would do. The Desoto acted as eager as any Desoto could. We pushed the top end, which was 89, and maybe 92 downhill. At that speed brakes don't give you much, so you'd better trust your steering and your tires.

If we passed The Dog we didn't know it. He might have parked in one of the towns, and of course we dropped a lot of revs passing through towns; that being neighborly. What with a little loafing, some pee stops, and general fooling around, we did not hit Minneapolis until a little after midnight. When we checked into a motel on the strip Potato was sleepy and grumpy. Chip looked relieved.

"Don't fall in love with that bed," Jesse told me. "Some damn salesman is out there waitin' to do us in. It pays to start early."

Car shopping with Jesse turned out as fascinating as anybody could expect. At 7 a.m. we cruised the lots. Cars stood in silent rows like advertising men lined up for group pictures. It being Minneapolis, we saw a lot of high-priced iron. Cadillacs and Packards and Lincolns sat beside Buick convertibles, hemi-Chryslers, and Corvettes ("nice c-hars," Jesse said about the Corvettes, "but no room to 'em. You couldn't carry more than one sack of feed.") Hudsons and Studebakers hunched along the back rows. On one lot was something called 'Classic Lane.' A Model A stood beside a '37 International pickup. An L29 Cord sat like a tombstone, which it was because it had no engine. But, glory be, beside the Cord nested a '39 LaSalle coupe just sparkling with threat. That LaSalle might have snookered Jesse, except something highly talented sat buried deep in the lot.

It was the last of the fast and elegant Lincolns, a '54 coupe as snarly as any man could want. The '53 model had taken the Mexican Road Race. The '54 was a refinement. After that, the marque went downhill. It started building cars for businessmen and rich grannies.

Jesse walked round and round the Lincoln, which looked like it was used to being cherished. Matchless and scratchless. It was a little less than fire engine red, with a white roof and a grill that could shrug off a cow. That Linc was a solid set of fixings. Jesse got soft lights in his eyes. This was no Miss Molly, but this was Miss somebody. There were a lot of crap crates running out there, but this Linc wasn't one of them.

"You prob'ly can't even get parts for the damn thing," Jesse murmured, and you could tell he was already scrapping with a salesman. He turned his back on the Lincoln. "We'll catch a bite to eat," he said. "This may take a couple days."

I felt sort of bubbly. "The Dog ain't gonna like this," I told Jesse.

"The Dog is gonna love it," he said. "Me and The Dog knows that road."

By the time the car lots opened at 9 a.m. Jesse had a trader's light in his eyes. About all that needs saying is that never before, or since, did I ever see a used car salesman cry.

The poor fellow never had a chance. He stood in his car lot most of the day while me and Jesse went through every car lot on the strip. We waved to him from a sweet little '57 Cad, and we cruised past real smooth in a mama-san '56 Imperial. We kicked tires on anything sturdy while he was watching, and we never even got to his lot until fifteen minutes before closing. Jesse and I climbed from my Desoto. Potato and Chip tailed after us.

"I always know when I get to Minneapolis," Jesse said to me, but loud enough the salesman could just about hear. "My woman wants to lay a farmer, and my dogs start pukin'." When we got within easy hearing range Jesse's voice got humble. "I expect this fella can help a cowboy in a fix."

I followed, experiencing considerable admiration. In two sentences Jesse had his man confused.

Potato was dumb enough that he trotted right up to the Lincoln. Chip sat and panted, pretending indifference. Then he ambled over to a ragged-out Pontiac and peed on the tire. "I must be missing something," Jesse said to the salesman, "because that dog has himself a dandy nose." He looked at the Pontiac. "This thing got an engine?"

We all conversed for the best part of an hour. Jesse refused to even look at the Lincoln. He sounded real serious about the LaSalle, to the point of running it around a couple of blocks. It was a darling. It had ceramic covered manifolds to protect against heat and rust. It packed a long stroke V8 with enough torque to bite rubber in second gear. My Desoto was a pretty thing, but until that LaSalle I never realized that my car was a total pussycat. When we left the lot the salesman looked sad. He was late for supper.

"Stay with what you've got," Jesse told me as he climbed in my Desoto. "The clock has run on that LaSalle. Let a collector have it. I hate it when something good dies for lack of parts." I wondered if he was thinking of Miss Molly.

"Because," Jesse said, and kicked the tire on a silly little Volkswagen, "the great, good cars are dying. I blame it on the Germans."

Next day we bought the Lincoln and made the salesman feel like one proud pup. He figured he foisted something off on Jesse that Jesse didn't want. He was so stuck on himself that he forgot that he had asked a thousand dollars, and come away with five-fifty. He even forgot that his eyes were swollen, and that maybe he crapped his pants.

We went for a test drive, but only after Jesse and I crawled around under the Linc. A little body lead lumped in the left rear fender, but the front end stood sound. Nobody had pumped any sawdust into the differential. We found no water in the oil, or oil in the water. The salesman stood around, admiring his shoeshine. He was one of those easterners who can't help talking down to people, especially when he's trying to be nice. I swear he wore a white tie with little red ducks on it. That Minnesota sunlight made his red hair blond, and his face pop with freckles.

Jesse drove real quiet until he found an interesting stretch of road. The salesman sat beside him. Me and Potato and Chip hunkered in the back seat. Chip looked sort of nauseated, but Potato was pretty happy.

"I'm afraid," Jesse said regretful, "that this thing is gonna turn out to be a howler. A fella gets a few years on him and he don't want a screamy car." Brother Jesse couldn't have been much more than thirty, but he tugged on his nose and ears like he was ancient. "I sure hope," he said real mournful, "that nobody stuck a boot in any of these here tires." Then he poured on some coal.

There was a most satisfying screech. That Linc took out like a roadrunner in heat. The salesman's head snapped backward, and his shoulders dug into the seat. Potato gave a happy, happy woof and stuck his nose out the open window. I felt like yelling hosannah, but knew enough to keep my big mouth shut. The Linc shrugged off a couple of cars that were conservatively motoring. It wheeled past a hay truck as the tires started humming. The salesman's freckles began to stand up like warts while the airstream howled. Old Potato kept his nose sticking through the open window and the wind kept drying it. Potato was so dam' dumb he tried to lick it wet while his nose stayed in the airstream. His tongue blew sideways.

"It ain't nothing but speed," Jesse complained. "Look at this here steering." He jogged the wheel considerable, which at ninety got even more considerable. The salesman's tie blew straight backward. The little red ducks matched his freckles. "Jee-sus-Chee-sus," he said, "Eight hundred and slow down." He braced himself against the dash.

When it hit the century mark the Linc developed a little float in the front end. I expect all of us were thinking about the tires.

You could tell Jesse was jubilant. The Linc still had some pedal left.

"I'm gettin' old," Jesse hollered above the wind. "This ain't no car for an old man."

"Seven hundred," the salesman said, "And Mother-of-God, slow it down."

"Five-fifty," Jesse told him, and dug the pedal down one more notch.

"You got it," the salesman hollered. His face twisted up real tear-y. Then Potato got all grateful and started licking the guy on the back of the neck.

So Jesse cut the speed and bought the Linc. He did it diplomatic, pretending he was sorry he'd made the offer. That was kind of him. After all, the guy was nothing but a used car salesman.

WE DID A SECOND NIGHT IN THAT MOTEL. THE LINC AND Desoto sat in an all-night filling station. Lube, oil change, and wash, because we were riding high. Jesse had a heap of money left over. In the morning we got new jeans and shirts, so as to ride along like gentlemen.

"We'll go back through South Dakota," Jesse told me. "There's a place I've heard about."

"What are we looking for?"

"We're checking on The Dog," Jesse told me, and would say no more.

We eased west to Bowman, just under the North Dakota line. Jesse sort of leaned into it, just taking joy from the whole occasion. I flowed along as best the Desoto could. Potato rode with Jesse, and Chip sat on the front seat beside me. Chip seemed rather easier in his mind.

A roadside cafe hunkered among tall trees. It didn't even have a neon sign. Real old-fashioned.

"I heard of this place all my life," Jesse said as he climbed from the Linc. "This here is the only outhouse in the world with a guest registry." He headed toward the rear of the cafe.

I tailed along, and Jesse, he was right. It was a palatial privvy built like a little cottage. The men's side was a three-holer. There was enough room for a standup desk. On the desk was one of those old-fashioned business ledgers like you used to see in banks.

"They're supposed to have a slew of these inside," Jesse said about the register as he flipped pages. "All the way back to the early days."

Some spirit of politeness seemed to take over when you picked up that register. There was hardly any bad talk. I read a few entries:

> On this site, May 16th, 1971, James John Johnson (John-John) cussed hell out of his truck.
>
> I came, I saw, I kinda liked it.
> —Bill Samuels, Tulsa
> This place does know squat.
> —Pauley Smith, Ogden
> This South Dakota ain't so bad, but I sure got the blues,
> I'm working in Tacoma,
> 'cause my kids all need new shoes.
> —Sad George

Brother Jesse flipped through the pages. "I'm even told," he said, "that Teddy Roosevelt crapped here. This is a fine old place." He sort of hummed as he flipped. "Uh, huh," he said, "The Dog done made his pee spot." He pointed to a page:

Road Dog
Run and run as fast as you can you can't catch me, I'm the Gingerbread Man.

Jesse just grinned. "He's sorta upping the ante, ain't he. You reckon this is getting serious?" Jesse acted like he knew what he was talking about, but I sure didn't.

II

We didn't know, as we headed home, that Jesse's graveyard business was about to take off. That wouldn't change him, though. He'd almost always had a hundred dollars in his jeans anyway, and was usually a happy man. What changed him was Road Dog and Miss Molly.

The trouble started a while after we crossed the Montana line. Jesse ran ahead in the Lincoln, and I tagged behind in my Desoto. We drove highway 2 into a western sunset. It was one of those magic summers where rain sweeps in from British Columbia just regular enough to keep things growing. Rabbits get fat and foolish, and foxes put on weight. Rattlesnakes come out of ditches to cross the sun-hot road. It's not sporting to run over their middles. You have to take them in the head. Redwings perch on fenceposts, and magpies flash black and white from the berm where they scavenge road kills

We saw a hell of a wreck just after Wolf Point. A guy in an old Kaiser came over the back of a rise and ran under a tanker truck that burned. Smoke rose black as a plume of crows, and we saw it five miles away. By the time we got there the truck driver stood in the middle of the road all white and shaking. The guy in the Kaiser sat behind the wheel. It was fearful to see how fast fire can work, and just terrifying to see bones hanging over a steering wheel. I remember thinking the guy no doubt died before any fire started, and we were feeling more than he was.

That didn't help. I said a prayer under my breath. The truck driver wasn't to blame, but he took it hard as a Presbyterian. Jesse tried to comfort him without much luck. The road melted and stank and began to burn. Nobody was drinking, but it was certain-sure we were all more sober than we'd ever been in our lives. Two deputies showed up. Cars drifted in easy, because of the smoke. In a couple of hours there were probably twenty cars lined up on either side of the wreck.

"He must have been asleep or drunk," Jesse said about the driver of the Kaiser. "How in hell can a man run under a tanker truck?"

When the cops reopened the road, night hovered over the plains. Nobody cared to run much over sixty, even beneath a bright moon. It seemed like a night to be superstitious; a night when there was a deer or pronghorn out there just ready to jump into your headlights. It wasn't a good night to drink, or shoot pool, or mess around in strange bars. It was a time for being home with your woman, if you had one.

On most nights ghosts do not show up beside the metal crosses, and they sure don't show up in owl light. Ghosts stand out on the darkest, moonless nights, and only then when bars are closed and the only thing open is the road.

I never gave it a thought. I chased Jesse's taillights, which on that Lincoln were broad up-and-down slashes in the dark. Chip sat beside me, sad and solemn. I rubbed his ears to perk him, but he just laid down and snuffled. Chip was sensitive. He knew I felt bad over that wreck.

The first ghost showed up on the left berm and fizzled before the headlights. It was a lady ghost, and a pretty old one judging from her long white hair and long white dress. She flicked on and off in just a flash, so maybe it was a road dream. Chip was so depressed he didn't even notice, and Jesse didn't either. His steering and his brakes didn't wave to me.

Everything stayed straight for another ten miles, then a whole peck of ghosts stood on the right berm. A bundle of crosses shone all silvery-white in the headlights. The ghosts melted into each other. You couldn't tell how many, but you could tell they were expectant. They looked like people lined up for a picture show. Jesse never gave a sign he saw them. I told myself to get straight. We hadn't had much sleep in the past two nights, and did some drinking the night before. We'd rolled near two thousand miles.

Admonishing seemed to work. Another twenty minutes passed, maybe thirty, and nothing happened. Wind chased through the open windows of the Desoto, and the radio gave mostly static. I kicked off my boots because that helps you stay awake; the bottoms of the feet being sensitive. Then a single ghost showed up on the right hand berm, and boy-howdy.

Why anybody would laugh while being dead has got to be a puzzle. This ghost was tall with Indian hair like Jesse's, and I could swear he looked like Jesse, the spitting image. This ghost was jolly. He clapped his hands and danced. Then he gave me the old road sign for 'roll 'em'; his hand circling in the air as he danced. The headlights penetrated him, showed tall grass solid at the roadside, and instead of legs he stood on a column of mist. Still, he was dancing.

It wasn't road dreams. It was hallucination. The nighttime road just fills with things seen or partly seen. When too much scary stuff happens, it's time to pull her over.

I couldn't do it, though. Suppose I pulled over, and suppose it wasn't hallucination? I recall thinking that a man don't ordinarily care for preachers until he needs one. It seemed like me and Jesse were riding through the Book of Revelations. I dropped my speed, then flicked my lights a couple times. Jesse paid it no attention, and then Chip got peculiar.

He didn't bark, he chirped. He stood up on the front seat, looking out the back window, and his paws trembled. He shivered, chirped, shivered, and went chirp, chirp, chirp. Headlights in back of us were closing fast.

I've been closed on plenty of times by guys looking for a ditch. Headlights have jumped out of night and fog and mist when nobody should be pushing forty. I've been overtaken by drunks

and suiciders. No set of headlights ever came as fast as the ones that began to wink in the mirrors. This highway 2 is a quick, quick road, but it's not the salt flats of Utah. The crazy man behind me was trying to set a new land speed record.

Never confuse an idiot. I stayed off the brakes and coasted, taking off speed and signaling my way onto the berm. The racer could have my share of the road. I didn't want any part of that boy's troubles. Jesse kept pulling away as I slowed. It seemed like he didn't even see the lights. Chip chirped, then sort of rolled down on the floorboards and cried.

For ninety seconds I feared being dead. For one second I figured it already happened. Wind banged the Desoto sideways. Wind whooped, the way it does in winter. The headlights blew past. What showed was the curve of a Hudson fender—the kind of curve you'd recognize if you'd been dead a million years—and what showed was the little squinchy shapes of a Hudson's taillights; and what showed was the slanty door post like a nail running kitty corner; and what showed was slivers of reflection from cracked glass on the rider's side; and what sounded was the drumbeat of a straight eight engine wanging like a locomotive gone wild; the thrump, bumpa, thrum of a crankshaft whipping in its bed. The slaunch-forward form of Miss Molly wailed, and showers of sparks blew from the tailpipe as Miss Molly rocketed.

Chip was not the only one howling. My voice rose high as the howl of Miss Molly. We all sang it out together, while Jesse cruised three, maybe four miles ahead. It wasn't two minutes before Miss Molly swept past that Linc like it was foundationed in cement. Sparks showered like the 4th of July, and Jesse's brake lights looked pale beside the fireworks. The Linc staggered against wind as Jesse headed for the berm. Wind smashed against my Desoto.

Miss Molly's taillights danced as she did a jig up the road, and then they winked into darkness as Miss Molly topped a rise, or disappeared. The night went darker than dark. A cloud scudded out of nowhere and blocked the moon.

Alongside the road the dancing ghost showed up in my headlights, and I could swear it was Jesse. He laughed like at a good joke, but he gave the old road sign for 'slow it down'; his hand palm down like he's patting an invisible pup. It seemed sound advice, and I blamed near liked him. After Miss Molly, a happy ghost seemed downright companionable.

"Shitfire," said Jesse, and that's all he said for the first five minutes after I pulled in behind him. I climbed from the

Desoto and walked to the Linc. Old Potato dog sprawled on the seat in a dead faint, and Jesse rubbed his ears trying to warm him back to consciousness. Jesse sat over the wheel like a man who has just met Jesus. His hand touched gentle on Potato's ears, and his voice sounded reverent. Brother Jesse's conversion wasn't going to last, but at the time it was just beautiful. He had the lights of salvation in his eyes, and his skinny shoulders weren't shaking too much. "I miss my c'har," he muttered finally, and blinked. He wasn't going to cry if he could help. "She's trying to tell me something," he whispered. "Let's find a bar. Miss Molly's in car heaven, certain sure."

We pulled away, found a bar, and parked. We drank some beer and slept across the car seats. Nobody wanted to go back on that road.

WHEN WE WOKE TO A MORNING HOT AND CLEAR, POTATO'S FUR had turned white. It didn't seem to bother him much, but for the rest of his life he was a lot more thoughtful.

"Looks like mashed Potato," Jesse said, but he wasn't talking a whole lot. We drove home like a couple of old ladies. Guys came scorching past, cussing at our granny-speed. We figured they could get mad and stay mad, or get mad and get over it. We made it back to Jesse's place about 2 in the afternoon.

A couple of things happened quick. Jesse parked beside his house trailer, and the front end fell out of the Lincoln. The right side went down, thump, and the right front tire sagged. Jesse turned even whiter than me, and I was bloodless. We had posted over a hundred miles an hour in that thing. Somehow, when we crawled around underneath inspecting it, we missed something. My shoulders and legs shook so hard I could barely get out of the Desoto. Chip was polite. He just yelped with happiness about being home, but he didn't trot across my lap as we climbed from the car.

Nobody could trust their legs. Jesse climbed out of the Linc and leaned against it. You could see him chewing over all the possibilities, then arriving at the only one that made sense. Some hammer mechanic bolted that front end together with no lock nut, no cotter pin, no lock washer, no lock-nothin'. He just wrenched down a plain old nut, and the nut worked loose.

"Miss Molly knew," Jesse whispered. "That's what she was trying to tell." He felt a lot better the minute he said it. Color came back to his face. He peered around the corner of the house trailer, looking toward Miss Molly's grave.

Mike Tarbush was over there with his '48 Roadmaster. Matt Simons stood beside him, and Matt's '56 Dodge sat beside the Roadmaster looking smug; which that model Dodge always did.

"I figger," Brother Jesse whispered, "that we should keep shut about last night. Word would just get around that we were alkies." He pulled himself together, arranged his face like a horse trying to grin, and walked toward the Roadmaster.

Mike Tarbush was a man in mourning. He sat on the fat trunk of that Buick and gazed off toward the mountains. Mike wore extra-large of everything, and still looked stout. He sported a thick red mustache to make up for his bald head. From time to time he bragged about his criminal record which amounted to three days in jail for assaulting a pool table. He threw it through a bar window.

Now his mustache drooped, and Mike seemed small inside his clothes. The hood of the Roadmaster gaped open. Under that hood things couldn't be worse. The poor thing had thrown a rod into the next county.

Jesse looked under the hood and tsked. "I know what you're going through," he said to Mike. He kind of petted the Roadmaster. "I always figured Betty Lou would last a century. What happened?"

There's no call to tell about a grown man blubbering, and especially not one who can heave pool tables. Mike finally got straight enough to tell the story.

"We was chasing The Dog," he said. "At least I think so. Three nights ago over to Kalispell. This Golden Hawk blew past me sittin'." Mike watched the distant mountains like he'd seen a miracle, or else like he was expecting one to happen. "That sonovabitch shore can drive," he whispered in disbelief. "Blown out by a dam' Studebaker."

"But a very swift Studebaker," Matt Simons said. Matt is as small as Mike is large, and Matt is educated. Even so, he's set his share of fenceposts. He looks like an algebra teacher, but not as delicate.

"Betty Lou went on up past her flat spot," Mike whispered. "She was tryin'. We had ninety on the clock, and The Dog left us sitting." He patted the Roadmaster. "I reckon she died of a broken heart."

"We got three kinds of funerals," Jesse said, and he was sympathetic. "We got the no-frills type, the regular-type, and the extra-special. The extra-special comes with flowers." He said it with a straight face, and Mike took it that way. He bought the extra-special, and that was sixty-five dollars.

Mike put up a nice marker:

1948–1961
Roadmaster two-door—Betty Lou
Gone to Glory while chasing The Dog
She was the best friend of Mike Tarbush

BROTHER JESSE WORKED ON THE LINCOLN UNTIL THE FRONT end tracked rock solid. He named it Sue Ellen, but not *Miss* Sue Ellen, there being no way to know if Miss Molly was jealous. When we examined Miss Molly's grave the soil seemed rumpled. Wildflowers, that Jesse sowed on the grave, bloomed in midsummer. I couldn't get it out of my head that Miss Molly was still alive, and maybe Jesse couldn't either.

Jesse explained about the Lincoln's name. "Sue Ellen is a lady I knew in Pocatello. I expect she misses me." He said it hopeful, like he didn't really believe it.

It looked to me like Jesse was brooding. Night usually found him in town, but sometimes he disappeared. When he was around he drove real calm and always got home before midnight. The wildness hadn't come out of Jesse, but he had it on a tight rein. He claimed he dreamed of Miss Molly. Jesse was working something out.

And so was I, awake or dreaming. Thoughts of the Road Dog filled my nights, and so did thoughts of the dancing ghost. As summer deepened, restlessness took me wailing under moonlight. The road unreeled before my headlights like a magic line that pointed to places under a warm sun where ladies laughed and fell in love. Something went wrong, though. During that summer the ladies stopped being dreams and became only imagination. When I told Jesse, he claimed I was just growing up. I wished for once Jesse was wrong. I wished for a lot of things, and one of the wishes came true. It was Mike Tarbush, not me, who got in the next tangle with Miss Molly.

Mike rode in from Billings where he'd been car shopping. He showed up at Jesse's place on Sunday afternoon. Montana lay restful. Birds hunkered on wires, or called from high grass.

Highway 2 ran watery with sunlight, deserted as a road ever could be. When Mike rolled a '56 Merc up beside the Linc it looked like old home week at a Ford dealership.

"I got to look at something," Mike said when he climbed from the Mercury. He sort of plodded over to Miss Molly's grave and hovered. Light breezes blew the wildflowers sideways. Mike looked like a bear trying to shake confusion from its head. He walked to the Roadmaster's grave. New grass sprouted reddish-green. "I was sober," Mike said. "Most Saturday nights, maybe I ain't, but I was sober as a deputy."

For a while nobody said anything. Potato sat glowing and white and thoughtful. Chip slept in the sun beside one of the tabbies. Then Chip woke up. He turned around three times and dashed to hide under the bulldozer.

"Now tell me I ain't crazy," Mike said. He perched on the front fender of the Merc, which was blue and white and adventuresome.

"Name of Judith," he said about the Merc. "A real lady." He swabbed sweat from his bald head. "I got blown out by Betty Lou and Miss Molly. That sound reasonable?" He swabbed some more sweat, and looked at the graves which stood like little speed bumps on the prairie. "Nope," he answered himself, "that don't sound reasonable a-tall."

"Something's wrong with your Mercury," Jesse said, real quiet. "You got a bad tire, or a hydraulic line about to blow, or something screwy in the steering."

He made Mike swear not to breathe a word. Then he told about Miss Molly and about the front end of the Lincoln. When the story got over, Mike looked like a halfback hit by a twelve man line.

"Don't drive another inch," Jesse said. "Not until we find what's wrong."

"That car already cracked a hundred," Mike whispered. "I bought it special to chase one sumbitch in a Studebaker." He looked toward Betty Lou's grave. "The Dog did that."

The three of us went through that Merc like men panning gold. The trouble was so obvious we missed it for two hours while the engine cooled. Then Jesse caught it. The fuel filter rubbed its underside against the valve cover. When Jesse touched it the filter collapsed. Gasoline spilled on the engine and the sparkplugs. That Merc was getting set to catch on fire.

"I got to wonder if The Dog did it," Jesse said about Betty Lou after Mike drove away. "I wonder if the Road Dog is the Studebaker type."

NIGHTS STARTED TO GET SERIOUS, BUT ANY LONESOMENESS ON that road was only in a man's head. As summer stretched past its longest days and sunsets started earlier, ghosts rose beside crosses before daylight hardly left the land. We drove to work and back, drove to town and back. My job was steady at a filling station, but it asked day after day of the same old thing. We never did any serious wrenching; no engine rebuilds or transmissions, just tuneups and flat tires. I dearly wanted to meet a nice lady, but no woman in her right mind would mess with a pump jockey.

Nights were different, though. I figured I was going crazy, and Jesse and Mike were worse. Jesse finally got his situation worked out. He claimed Miss Molly was protecting him. Jesse and Mike took the Linc and the Merc on long runs, just wringing the howl out of those cars. Some nights they'd flash past me at speeds no sane man would try in darkness. Jesse was never a real big drinker, and Mike stopped altogether. They were too busy playing road games. It got so the state cop never tried to chase them. He just dropped past Jesse's place next day and passed out tickets.

The dancing ghost danced in my dreams, both asleep and driving. When daylight left the land I passed metal crosses and remembered some of the wrecks.

Three crosses stood on one side of the railroad track, and four crosses on the other side. The three happened when some Canadian cowboys lost a race with a train. It was too awful to remember, but on most nights those guys stood looking down the tracks with startled eyes.

The four crosses happened when one-third of the senior class of '59 hit that grade too fast on prom night. They rolled a damned old Chevrolet. More bodies by Fisher. Now the two girls stood in their long dresses looking wistful. The two boys pretended that none of it meant nothin'.

Further out the road things had happened before my time. An Indian ghost most often stood beside the ghost of a deer. In another place a chubby old rancher looked real picky and angry.

The dancing ghost continued unpredictable. All the other ghosts stood beside their crosses, but the dancing ghost showed up anywhere he wanted, anytime he wanted. I'd slow the Desoto as he came into my lights, and he was the spitting image of Jesse.

"I don't want to hear about it," Jesse said when I tried to tell him. "I'm on a roll. I'm even gettin' famous."

He was right about that. People up and down the line joked about Jesse and his graveyard business.

"It's the very best kind of advertising," he told me. "We'll see more action before snow flies."

"You won't see snow fly," I told him, standing up to him a second time. "Unless you slow down and pay attention."

"I've looked at heaps more road than you," he told me, "and seeing things is just part of the night. That nighttime road is different."

"This is starting to happen at last light."

"I don't see no ghosts," he told me, and he was lying. "Except Miss Molly once or twice." He wouldn't say anything more.

And Jesse was right. As summer ran on more graves showed up near Miss Molly. A man named Mcguire turned up with a '41 Cad.

1941–1961
Fleetwood Coupe—Annie
304,018 miles on flathead V8
She was the luck of the Irishman
Pat Mcguire

And Sam Winder buried his '47 Packard.

1947–1961
Packard 2-door—Lois Lane
Super Buddy of Sam Winder Up Up and Away

And Pete Johansen buried his pickup.

1946–1961
Ford pickup — Gertrude
211,000 miles give or take Never a screamer but a good pulling truck.
Pete Johansen put up many a day's work with her.

MONTANA ROADS ARE LONG AND LONESOME, AND ALONG THE highline is lonesomest of all. From Saskatchewan to Texas nothing stands tall enough to break the wind which begins to blow cold and clear toward late October. Rains sob away toward the middlewest, and grass turns goldish-amber.

Rattlesnakes move to high ground where they will winter. Every creature on God's plains begins to fat-up against the winter. Soon it's going to be 30 below and the wind blowing.

Four wheel drive weather. Internationals and Fords, with Dodge crummy-wagons in the hills; cars and trucks will line up beside houses, garages, sheds, with electric wires leading from plugs to radiators and blocks. They look like packs of nursing pups. Work will slow, then stop. New work turns to accounting for the weather. Fuel, emergency generators, hay bale insulation. Horses and cattle and deer look fuzzy beneath thick coats. Check your battery. If your rig won't start, and you two miles from home, she won't die—but you might.

School buses creep from stop to stop, and bundled kids look like colorful little bears trotting through late afternoon light. Snowy owls come floating in from northward, while folks go to church on Sunday against the time when there's some better amusement. Men hang around town, because home is either empty or crowded, depending on if you're married. Folks sit before television watching the funny, goofy, unreal world where everybody plays at being sexy and naked, even when they're not.

And 19 years old is lonesome, too. And work is lonesome when nobody much cares for you.

BEFORE WINTER SET IN, I GOT IT IN MY HEAD TO RUN THE ROAD Dog's route. It was September. Winter would close us down pretty quick. The trip would be a luxury. What with room rent, and gas, and eating out, it was payday to payday with me. Still, one payday would account for gas and sandwiches. I could sleep across the seat. I hocked a Marlin 30-30 to Jesse for twenty bucks. He seemed happy with my notion. He even went into the greenhouse and came out with an arctic sleeping bag.

"In case things get vigorous," he said, and grinned. "Now get on out there and bite The Dog."

It was a happy time. Dreams of ladies sort of set themselves to one side as I cruised across the eternal land. I came to love the land that autumn, in a way that maybe ranchers do. The land stopped being something that a road ran across. Canadian honkers came winging in vees from the north. The great Montana sky stood easy as eagles. When I'd pull over and cut the engine, sounds of grasshoppers mixed with birdcalls. Once, a wild turkey, as smart as any domestic turkey is dumb, talked to himself and paid me not the least mind. The Dog showed up right away. In a cafe in Malta:

Road Dog
"It was all a hideous mistake."
—Christopher Columbus

In a bar in Tampico:

Road Dog
Who's afraid of the big bad Woof?

In another bar in Culbertson:

Road Dog
Go East young man, go East

I rolled Williston and dropped south through North Dakota. The Dog's trail disappeared until Watford City where it showed up in the can of a filling station:

Road Dog
Atlantis and Sargasso
Full fathom five thy brother lies

And in a joint in Grassy Butte:

Road Dog
Ain't Misbehavin'

That morning in Grassy Butte I woke to a sunrise where the land lay bathed in rose and blue. Silhouettes of grazing deer mixed with silhouettes of cattle. They herded together peaceful as a dream of having your own place, your own woman, and you working hard; and her glad to see you coming home.

In Bowman The Dog showed up in a nice restaurant:

Road Dog
The Katzenjammer Kids minus one

Ghosts did not show up along the road, but the road stayed the same. I tangled with a bathtub Hudson, a '53, outside of Spearfish in South Dakota. I chased him into Wyoming like being dragged on a string. The guy played with me for twenty miles, then got bored. He shoved more coal in the stoker and purely flew out of sight.

Sheridan was a nice town back in those days, just nice and friendly; plus I started to get sick of the way I smelled. In early afternoon I found a five dollar motel with a shower. That gave me the afternoon, the evening, and next morning if it seemed right. I spiffed up, put on a good shirt, slicked down my hair and felt just fine.

The streets lay dusty and lazy. Rancher's pickups stood all dented and workworn before bars, and an old Indian sat on hay bales in the back of one of them. He wore a flop hat, and he seemed like the eyes and heart of the prairie. He looked at me like I was a splendid puppy that might someday amount to something. It seemed okay when he did it.

I hung around a soda fountain at the five and dime because a girl smiled. She was just beautiful. A little horsey-faced, but with sun-blond hair, and with hands long-fingered and gentle. There wasn't a chance of talking because she stood behind the counter for lady's underwear. I pretended to myself that she looked sad when I left.

It got onto late afternoon. Sunlight drifted in between buildings, and shadows overreached the streets. Everything was normal, and then everything got scary.

I was just poking along, looking in store windows, checking the show at the movie house, when ahead of me Jesse walked toward a Golden Hawk. He was maybe a block and a half away, but it was Jesse sure as God made sunshine. It was a Golden Hawk. There was no way of mistaking that car. Hawks were high-priced sets of wheels, and Studebaker never sold that many.

I yelled and ran. Jesse waited beside the car looking sort of puzzled. When I pulled up beside him he grinned.

"It's happening again," he said, and his voice sounded amused but not mean. Sunlight made his face reddish, but shadow put his legs and feet in darkness. "You believe me to be a gentleman named Jesse Still." Behind him shadows of buildings told that night was on its way. Sunset happens quick on the prairies.

And I said, "Jesse, what in the hell are you doing in Sheridan?"

And he said, "Young man, you are not looking at Jesse Still." He said it quiet and polite, and he thought he had a point. His voice was smooth and cultured, so he sure didn't sound like Jesse. His hair hung combed-out, and he wore clothes that never came from a drygoods. His jeans were soft looking and expensive. His boots were tooled. They kind of glowed in the dusk. The Golden Hawk didn't have a dust speck on it, and the interior had never carried a tool, or a car part, or a sack of feed. It just sparkled. I almost believed him, and then I didn't.

"You're fooling with me."

"On the contrary," he said real soft, "Jesse Still is fooling with *me*, although he doesn't mean to. We've never met." He didn't exactly look nervous, but he looked impatient. He climbed in the Stude and started the engine. It purred like racing tune. "This is a large and awfully complex world," he said, "and Mr. Still will probably tell you the same. I've been told we look like brothers."

I wanted to say more, but he waved real friendly and pulled away. The flat and racey backend of the Hawk reflected one slash of sunlight, then rolled into shadow. If I'd had a hot car I'd have gone out hunting him. It wouldn't have done a lick of good, but doing something would be better than doing nothing.

I stood sort of shaking and amazed. Life had just changed somehow, and it wasn't going to change back. There wasn't a thing in the world to do, so I went to get some supper. The Dog had signed in at the cafe:

Road Dog
The Bobbsey Twins Attend The Motor Races

And—I sat chewing roast beef and mashed potatoes.

And—I saw how the guy in the Hawk might be lying, and that Jesse was a twin.

And—I finally saw what a chancy, dicey world this was, because without meaning to, exactly; and without even knowing it was happening, I had just run up against the Road Dog.

IT WAS A NIGHT OF DREAMS. DREAMS WOULDN'T LET ME GO. The dancing ghost tried to tell me Jesse was triplets. The ghosts among the crosses begged rides into nowhere, rides down the long tunnel of night that ran past lands of dreams but never turned off to those lands. It all came back, the crazy summer, the running, running, running behind the howl of engines. The Road Dog drawled with Jesse's voice, and then The Dog spoke cultured. The girl at the five and dime held out a gentle hand, then pulled it back. I dreamed of a hundred roadside joints, bars, cafes, old-fashioned filling stations with grease pits. I dreamed of winter wind, and the dark, dark days of winter; and of nights when you hunch in your room because it's a chore too big to bundle up and go outside.

I woke to an early dawn and slurped coffee at the bakery which kept open because they had to make morning donuts. The land lay all around me, but it had nothing to say. I counted my money and

figured miles.

I climbed in the Desoto thinking I had never got around to giving it a name. The road unreeled toward the west. It ended in Seattle where I sold my car. Everybody said there was going to be a war, and I wasn't doing anything, anyway. I joined the Navy.

III

What with him burying cars and raising hell, Jesse never wrote to me in summer. He was surely faithful in winter, though. He wrote long letters printed in a clumsy hand. He tried to cheer me up, and so did Matt Simons.

The Navy sent me to boot camp and diesel school, then to a motor pool in San Diego. I worked there three and a half years, sometimes even working on ships if the ships weren't going anywhere. A sunny land and smiling ladies lay all about, but the ladies mostly fell in love by ten at night and got over it by dawn. Women in the bars were younger and prettier than back home. There was enough clap to go around.

"The business is growing like jimson weed," Jesse wrote toward Christmas of '62. "I buried fourteen cars this summer, and one of them was a kraut." He wrote a whole page about his morals. It didn't seem right to stick a crap crate in the ground beside real cars. At the same time it was bad business not to. He opened a special corner of the cemetery and pretended it was exclusive for foreign iron.

"And Mike Tarbush got to drinking," he wrote. "I'm sad to say we planted Judith."

Mike never had a minute's trouble with that Merc. Judith behaved like a perfect lady until Mike turned upside down. He backed across a parking lot at night, rather hasty, and drove backwards up the guywire of a power pole. It was the only rollover wreck in history that happened at twenty miles an hour.

"Mike can't stop discussing it," Jesse wrote. "He's never caught The Dog, neither, but he ain't stopped trying. He wheeled in here in a beefed up '57 Olds called Sally. It goes like stink and looks like a hereford."

Home seemed far away, though it couldn't have been more than thirty-six hours by road for a man willing to hang over the wheel. I wanted to take a leave and drive home, but knew it better not happen. Once I got there I'd likely stay.

"George Pierson at the feed store says he's going to file a paternity suit against Potato," Jesse wrote. "The pups are cute and there's a family resemblance."

It came to me then why I was homesick. I surely missed the land, but even more I missed the people. Back home folks were important enough that you knew their names. When somebody got messed up or killed you felt sorry. In California nobody knew nobody. They just swept up broken glass and moved right along. I should have meshed right in. I had made my rating and was pushing a rich man's car, a '57 hemi Chrysler; but never felt it fit.

"Don't pay it any mind," Jesse wrote when I told about meeting Road Dog. "I've heard about a guy who looks the same as me. Sometimes stuff like that happens." And, that was all he ever did say.

1963 ended happy and hopeful. Matt Simons wrote
a letter. Sam Winder bought a big Christmas card and
everybody signed it with little messages. Even my old boss at
the filling station signed 'Merry Xmas Jed—Keep It Between
The Fenceposts.' My boss didn't hold it against me that I left.
In Montana a guy is supposed to be free to find out what he's
all about.

Christmas of '63 saw Jesse pleased as a bee in clover. A
lady named Sarah moved in with him. She waitressed at the
cafe, and Jesse's letter ran pretty short. He'd put twenty-three
cars under that year, and bought more acreage. He ordered
a genuine marble gravestone for Miss Molly. "Sue Ellen is a
real darling," Jesse wrote about the Linc. "That marker like-
to weighed a ton. We just about bent a back axle bringing it
from the railroad."

From Christmas of '63 to January of '64 was just a few
days, but they marked an awful downturn for Jesse. His letter
was more real to me than all the diesels in San Diego.

He drew black borders all around the pages. The letter
started out okay, but went downhill. "Sarah moved out and
into a rented room," he wrote. "I reckon I was just too much
to handle." He didn't explain, but I did my own reckoning.
I could imagine that it was Jesse, plus two cats and two dogs
trying to get into a ten-wide-fifty trailer, that got to Sarah. "I
think she misses me," he wrote, "but I expect she'll have to
bear it."

Then the letter got just awful.

"A pack of wolves came through from Canada," Jesse
wrote. "They picked off old Potato like a berry from a bush.
Me and Mike found tracks, and a little blood in the snow."

I sat in the summery dayroom surrounded by sailors
shooting pool and playing ping pong. I imagined the snow
and ice of home. I imagined old Potato nosing around in his

dumb and happy way, looking for rabbits, or lifting his leg. Maybe he even wagged his tail when that first wolf came into view. I sat blinking tears, ready to bawl over a dog, and then I did, and to hell with it.

The world was changing and it wouldn't change back. I put in for sea duty one more time, and the Chief Warrant who ramrodded that motor pool turned it down again. He claimed we kept the world safe by wrenching engines.

"The '62 Dodge is emerging as the car of choice for people in a hurry." Matt Simons wrote that in February '64, knowing I'd understand that nobody could tell which cars would be treasured until they had a year or two on them. "It's an extreme winter," he wrote, "and it's taking its toll on many of us. Mike has now learned not to punch a policeman. He's doing ten days. Sam Winder managed to roll a Jeep, and neither he, nor I, can figure out how a man can roll a Jeep. Sam has a broken arm, and lost two toes to frost. He was trapped under the wreck. It took awhile to pull him out. Brother Jesse is in the darkest sort of mood. He comes and goes in an irregular manner, but the Linc sits outside the pool hall on most days.

"And for myself," Matt wrote, "I think come summer I'll drop some revs. My flaming youth seems to be giving way to other interests. A young woman named Nancy started teaching at the school. Until now I thought I was a confirmed bachelor."

A postcard came the end of February. The postmark said Cheyenne, Wyoming, way down in the southeast corner of the state. It was written fancy. Nobody could mistake that fine, spidery hand. It read:

Road Dog
Run and run as fast as he can, He can't find who is the Gingerbread Man

The picture on the card had been taken from an airplane. It showed an oval racetrack where cars chased each other round and round. I couldn't figure why Jesse sent it, but it had to be Jesse. Then it came to me that Jesse was the Road Dog. Then it came to me that he wasn't. The Road Dog was too slick. He wrote real delicate, and Jesse only printed real clumsy. On the other hand, the Road Dog didn't know me from Adam's off ox. Somehow it *had* to be Jesse.

"We got snow nut-deep to a tall palm tree," Jesse wrote at about the same time, "and Chip is failing. He's off his feed. He don't even tease the kitties. Chip just can't seem to stop mourning."

I had bad premonitions. Chip was sensitive. I feared he wouldn't be around by the time I got back home, and my fear proved right. Chip held off until the first warm sun of spring and then he died while napping in the shade of the bulldozer. When Jesse sent a quick note telling me, I felt pretty bad, but had been expecting it. Chip had a good heart. I figured now he was with Potato, romping in the hills somewhere. I knew that was a bunch of crap, but that's just the way I chose to figure it.

THEY SAY A MAN CAN GET USED TO ANYTHING, BUT MAYBE SOME can't. Day after day, and week after week, California weather nagged. Sometimes a puny little dab of weather dribbled in from the Pacific, and people hollered it was storming. Sometimes temperatures dropped toward the fifties, and people trotted around in thick sweaters and coats. It was almost a relief when that happened, because everybody put on their shirts. In three years I'd seen more woman-skin than a normal man sees in a lifetime, and more tattoos on men. The Chief Warrant at the motor pool had the only tattoo in the world called 'worm's eye view of a pig's butt in the moonlight'.

In autumn '64, with one more year to pull, I took a two week leave and headed north just chasing weather. It showed up first in Oregon with rain, and more in Washington. I got hassled on the Canadian border by a distressful little guy who thought, what with the war, that I wanted political asylum.

I chased on up to Calgary where matters got chill and wholesome. Wind worked through the mountains, like it wanted to drive me south toward home. Elk and moose and porcupines went about their business. Red tail hawks circled. I slid on over to Edmonton, chased on east to Saskatoon, then dropped south through the Dakotas. In Williston I had a terrible want to cut and run for home, but didn't dare.

The Road Dog showed up all over the place, but the messages were getting strange. At a bar in Amidon:

Road Dog
Taking Kentucky Windage

At a hamburger joint in Belle Fourche:

Road Dog
Chasing his tail

At a restaurant in Redbird:

Road Dog
Flea and flee as much as we can
We'll soon find who is the Gingerbread Man

In a pool room in Fort Collins:

Road Dog
Home home on derange

Road Dog, or Jesse, was too far south. The Dog had never showed up in Colorado before. At least nobody ever heard of such. My leave was running out. There was nothing to do except sit over the wheel. I dropped on south to Albuquerque, hung a right, and headed back to the big city. All along the road I chewed a dreadful fear for Jesse. Something bad was happening, and that didn't seem fair because something good went on between me and the Chrysler. We reached an understanding. The Chrysler came alive and began to hum. All that poor car had ever needed was to look at road. It had been raised among traffic and poodles, but needed long sight-distances and bears.

WHEN I GOT BACK, THERE SEEMED NO WAY OUT OF WRITING A letter to Matt Simons, even if it was borrowing trouble. It took evening after evening of gnawing the end of a pencil. I hated to tell about Miss Molly, and about the dancing ghost, and about my fears for Jesse. A man is supposed to keep his problems to himself.

At the same time, Matt was educated. Maybe he could give Jesse a hand if he knew all of it. The letter came out pretty thick. I mailed it thinking Matt wasn't likely to answer real soon. Autumn deepened to winter back home, and everybody would be busy.

So I worked and waited. There was an old White Mustang with a fifth wheel left over from the last war. It was a lean and hungry looking animal, and slightly marvelous. I overhauled the engine, then dropped the tranny and adapted a tenspeed Roadranger. When I got that truck running smooth as a Baptist's mouth, the Navy surveyed it and sold it for scrap.

"Ghost cars are a tradition," Matt wrote toward the back of October, "and I'd be hard pressed to say they are not real.

I recall being passed by an Auburn boat-tail about 3 a.m. on a summer day. That happened ten years ago. I was about your age, which means there was not an Auburn boat-tail in all of Montana. That car died in the early '30s.

"And we all hear stories of huge old headlights overtaking in the mist; stories of Mercers and Duesenbergs and Bugattis. I try to believe the stories are true, because, in a way, it would be a shame if they were not.

"The same for road ghosts. I've never seen a ghost who looked like Jesse. The ghosts I've seen might not have been ghosts. To paraphrase an expert, they may have been a trapped beer-belch, an undigested hamburger, or blowing mist. On the other hand, maybe not. They certainly seemed real at the time.

"As for Jesse—we have a problem here. In a way we've had it for a long while, but only since last winter have matters become solemn. Then your letter arrives and matters become mysterious. Jesse has— or had—a twin brother. One night when we were carousing he told me that, but he also said his brother was dead. Then he swore me to a silence I must now break."

Matt went on to say that I must never, never say anything. He figured something was going on between brothers. He figured it must run deep.

"There is something uncanny about twins," Matt wrote. "What great matters are joined in the womb? When twins enter the world they learn and grow the way all of us do; but some communication (or communion) surely happens before birth. A clash between brothers is a terrible thing. A clash between twins may spell tragedy."

Matt went on to tell how Jesse was going over the edge with road games, only the games stayed close to home. All during the summer Jesse would head out, roll fifty or a hundred miles, and come home scorching like drawn by a string. Matt guessed the postcard I'd gotten from Jesse in February was part of the game, and it was the last time Jesse had been very far from home. Matt figured Jesse used tracing paper to imitate the Road Dog's writing. He also figured Road Dog had to be Jesse's brother.

"It's obvious," Matt wrote, "that Jesse's brother is still alive, and is only metaphorically dead to Jesse. There are look-alikes in this world, but you have reported identical twins."

Matt told how Jesse drove so crazy even Mike would not run with him. That was bad enough, but it seemed the graveyard had sort of moved in on Jesse's mind. That graveyard was no longer just something to do. Jesse swapped around until he came up with a tractor and mower. Three times that summer he trimmed the graveyard and straightened markers. He dusted and polished Miss Molly's headstone.

"It's past being a joke," Matt wrote, "or a sentimental indulgence. Jesse no longer drinks, and no longer hells around in a general way. He either runs road or tends the cemetery. I've seen other men search for a ditch, but never in such bizarre fashion."

Jesse had been seen on his knees praying before Miss Molly's grave.

"Or perhaps he was praying for himself, or for Chip," Matt wrote. "Chip is buried beside Miss Molly. The graveyard has to be seen to be believed. Who would ever think so many machines would be so dear to so many men?"

Then Matt went on to say he was going to 'inquire in various places' that winter. "There are ways to trace Jesse's brother," Matt wrote, "and I am very good at that sort of research." He said it was about the only thing he could still do for Jesse.

"Because," Matt wrote, "I seem to have fallen in love with a romantic. Nancy wants a June wedding. I look forward to another winter alone, but it will be an easy wait. Nancy is rather old-fashioned, and I find that I'm old-fashioned as well. I will never regret my years spent helling around, but am glad they are now in the past."

Back home winter deepened. At Christmas a long letter came from Jesse and some of it made sense. "I put 18 cars under this summer. Business fell off because I lost my hustle. You got to scooch around a good bit, or you don't make contacts. I may start advertising.

"And the tabbies took off. I forgot to slop them regular, so now they're mousing in a barn on Jimmy Come Lately Road. Mike says I ought to get another dog, but my heart ain't in it."

Then the letter went into plans for the cemetery. Jesse talked some grand ideas. He thought a nice wrought iron gate might be showy, and bring in business. He thought of finding a truck that would haul 'deceased' cars. "On the other hand," he wrote, "if a guy don't care enough to find a tow, maybe I don't want to plant his iron." He went on for a good while about morals, but a lawyer couldn't understand it. He seemed to be saying something about respect for Miss Molly, and Betty Lou, and Judith. "Sue Ellen is a real hummer," he wrote about the Linc. "She's got two hundred thousand I know about, plus whatever went on before."

Which meant Jesse was piling up about seventy thousand miles a year, and that didn't seem too bad. Truck drivers put up a hundred thousand. Of course, they make a living at it.

Then the letter got so crazy it was hard to credit.

"I got the Road Dog figured out. There's two little kids. Their mama reads to them and they play tag. The one that don't get caught gets to be the Gingerbread Man. This all come together because I ran across a bunch of kids down on the Colorado line. I was down that way to call on a lady I once knew but she moved and I said what the hell and hung around a few days and that's what clued me to The Dog. The kids were at a Sunday School picnic, and I was napping across the carseat. Then a preacher's wife came over and saw I wasn't drunk, but the preacher was there too, and they invited me. I eased over to the picnic and everybody made me welcome. Anyway, those kids were playing, and I heard the gingerbread business, and I figure The Dog is from Colorado."

The last page of the letter was just as scary. Jesse took kids' crayons and drew the front ends of the Linc and Miss Molly. There was a tail that was probably Potato's, sticking out from behind the picture of Miss Molly, and everything was centered around the picture of a marker that said R.I.P. Road Dog.

But—there weren't any little kids. Jesse had not been to Colorado. Jesse had been tending that graveyard, and staying close to home. Jesse played make-believe, or else Matt Simons lied; and there was no reason for Matt to lie. Something bad, bad wrong was going on with Jesse.

There was no help for it. I did my time and wrote a letter every month or six weeks pretending everything was normal. I wrote about what we'd do when I got home, and about the Chrysler. Maybe that didn't make much sense, but Jesse was important to me. He was a big part of what I remembered about home.

At the end of April a postcard came, this time from Havre. "The Dog is after me. I feel it." It was just a plain old postcard. No picture.

Matt wrote in May, mostly his own plans. He busied himself building a couple of rooms onto his place. "Nancy and I do not want a family right away," he wrote, "but someday we will." He wrote a bubbly letter, with a feel of springtime to it.

"I almost forgot my main reason for writing," the letter said. "Jesse comes from around Boulder, Colorado. His parents are long dead, ironically in a car wreck. His mother was a schoolteacher, his father a librarian. Those people, who lived such quiet lives, somehow produced a hellion like Jesse, and Jesse's brother. That's the factual side of the matter.

"The human side is so complex it will not commit to paper. In fact, I do not trust what I know. When you get home next fall we'll discuss it."

The letter made me sad and mad. Sad because I wasn't getting married, and mad because Matt didn't think I'd keep my mouth shut. Then I thought better of it. Matt didn't trust himself. I did what any gentleman would do, and sent him and Nancy a nice gravy boat for the wedding.

In late July Jesse sent another postcard. "He's after me, I'm after him. If I ain't around when you get back don't fret. Stuff happens. It's just a matter of chasing road."

Summer rolled on. The Navy released 'non essential personnel' in spite of the war. I put four years in the outfit and got called nonessential. Days choked past like a rig with fouled injectors. One good thing happened. My old boss moved his station to the outskirts of town and started an IH dealership. He straight-out wrote how he needed a diesel mechanic. I felt hopeful thoughts, and dark ones.

In September I became a veteran who qualified for an overseas ribbon, because of work on ships that later on went somewhere. Now I could join the Legion Post back home, which was maybe the pay-off. They had the best pool table in the county.

"Gents," I said to the boys at the motor pool, "it's been a distinct by-God pleasure enjoying your company, and don't never come to Montana 'cause she's a heartbreaker." The Chrysler and me lit out like a kyoodle of pups.

It would have been easier to run Salt Lake, then climb the map to Havre, but notions pushed. I slid east to Las Cruces then popped north to Boulder with the idea of tracing Jesse. The Chrysler hummed and chewed up road. When I got to Boulder the notion turned hopeless. There were too many people. I didn't even know where to start asking.

It's no big job to fool yourself. Above Boulder it came to me how I've been pointing for Sheridan all along, and not even Sheridan. I pointed toward a girl who smiled at me four years ago.

I found her working at a hardware, and she wasn't wearing any rings. I blushed around a little bit, then got out of there to catch my breath. I thought of how Jesse took whatever time was needed when he bought the Linc. It looked like this would take a while.

My pockets were crowded with mustering out pay and money for unused leave. I camped in a ten dollar motel. It took three days to get acquainted, then we went to a show and supper afterward. Her name was Linda. Her father was a Mormon. That meant a year of courting, but it's not all that far from North Montana to Sheridan.

I had to get home and get employed, which would make the Mormon happy. On Saturday afternoon, Linda and I went back to the same old movie, but this time we held hands. Before going home she kissed me once, real gentle. That made up for those hard times in San Diego. It let me know I was back with my own people.

I drove downtown all fired-up with visions. It was way too early for bed, and I cared nothing for a beer. A run down cafe sat on the outskirts. I figured pie and coffee.

The Dog had signed in. His writing showed faint, like the wall had been scrubbed. Newer stuff scrabbled over it.

Road Dog
Tweedle Dum and Tweedle Dee
Lonely pups as pups can be
For each other had to wait
Down beside the churchyard gate

The cafe sort of slumbered. Several old men lined the counter. Four young gearheads sat at a table and talked fuel injection. The old men yawned and put up with it. Faded pictures of old racing cars hung along the walls. The young guys sat beneath a picture of the Bluebird. That car held the land speed record of 301.29 m.p.h. This was a racer's cafe, and had been for a long, long time.

The waitress was graying and motherly. She tsked and tished over the old men as much as she did the young ones. Her eyes held that long-distance prairie look, a look knowing wind and fire and hard times; stuff that either breaks people or leaves them wise. Matt Simons might get that look in another twenty years. I tried to imagine Linda when she became the waitress' age, and it wasn't bad imagining.

Pictures of quarter-mile cars hung back of the counter, and pictures of street machines hung on each side of the door. '50's hotrods scorched beside worked-up stockers. Some mighty rowdy iron crowded that wall. One picture showed a Golden Hawk. I walked over, and in one corner was the name 'Still'—written in the Road Dog's hand. It shouldn't have been scary.

I went back to the counter shaking. A nice looking old gent nursed coffee. His hands wore knuckles busted by a thousand slipped wrenches. Grease was worked-in deep around his eyes, the

way it gets after years and years when no soap made will touch it. You could tell he'd been a steady man. His eyes were clear as a kid.

"Mister," I said, "and beg pardon for bothering you. Do you know anything about that Studebaker?" I pointed to the wall.

"You ain't bothering me," he said, "but I'll tell you when you do." He tapped the side of his head like trying to ease a gear in place, then he started talking engine specs on the Stude.

"I mean the man who owns it."

The old man probably liked my haircut, which was short. He liked it that I was raised right. Young guys don't always pay old men much mind.

"You still ain't bothering me." He turned to the waitress. "Sue," he said, "has Johnny Still been in?"

She turned from cleaning the pie case, and she looked toward the young guys like she feared for them. You could tell she was no big fan of engines. "It's been the better part of a year, maybe more." She looked down the line of old men. "I was fretting about him just the other day . . ." She let it hang. Nobody said anything. "He comes and goes so quiet, you might miss him."

"I don't miss him a hell of a lot," one of the young guys said. The guy looked like a duck, and had a voice like a sparrow. His fingernails were too clean. That proved something.

"Because Johnny blew you out," another young guy said. "Johnny *always* blew you out."

"Because he's crazy," the first guy said. "There's noisy-crazy and quiet-crazy. The guy is a spook."

"He's going through something," the waitress said, and said it kind. "Johnny's taken a lot of loss. He's the type who grieves." He looked at me like she expected an explanation.

"I'm friends with his brother," I told her. "Maybe Johnny and his brother don't get along."

The old man looked at me rather strange. "You go back quite a-ways," he told me. "Jesse's been dead a good long time."

I thought I'd pass out. My hands started shaking, and my legs felt too weak to stand. Beyond the window of the cafe red light came from a neon sign, and inside the cafe everybody sat quiet

waiting to see if I was crazy too. I sort of picked at my pie. One of the young guys moved real uneasy. He loafed toward the door, maybe figuring he'd need a shotgun. The other three young ones looked confused.

"No offense," I said to the old man, "but Jesse Still is alive. Up on the highline. We run together."

"Jesse Still drove a damn old Hudson Terraplane into the South Platte River in spring of '52, maybe '53." The old man said it real quiet. "He popped a tire when not real sober."

"Which is why Johnny doesn't drink," the waitress said. "At least I expect that's the reason."

"And now you are bothering me." The old man looked to the waitress, and she was as full of questions as he was.

Nobody ever felt more hopeless or scared. These folks had no reason to tell this kind of yarn. "Jesse is sort of roughhouse." My voice was only whispering. It wouldn't make enough sound. "Jesse made his reputation helling around."

"You've got that part right," the old man told me, "and youngster, I don't give a tinker's dam if you believe me or not, but Jesse Still is dead."

I saw what it had to be, but seeing isn't always believing. "Thank you, mister," I whispered to the old man, "and thank you ma'am," to the waitress. Then I hauled out of there leaving them with something to discuss.

A TERRIBLE FEAR ROLLED WITH ME, BECAUSE OF JESSE'S LAST postcard. He said he might not be home, and now that could mean more than it said. The Chrysler bettered its reputation, and we just flew. From the Montana line to Shelby is eight hours on a clear day. You can wail it in seven, or maybe six and a half if a deer doesn't tangle with your front end. I was afraid, and confused, and getting mad. Me and Linda were just to the point of hoping for an understanding, and now I was going to get killed running over a porcupine or into a heifer. The Chrysler blazed like a hound on a hot scent. At eighty, the pedal kept wanting to dig deep and really howl.

The nighttime road yells danger. Shadows crawl over everything. What jumps into your headlights may be real, and maybe not. Metal crosses hold little clusters of dark flowers on their arms, and the land rolls out beneath the moon. Buttes stand like great ships anchored in the plains, and riverbeds run like dry ink. Come spring they'll flow, but in September all flow is in the road.

The dancing ghost picked me up on highway 3 outside Comanche, but this time he wasn't dancing. He stood on the berm and no mist tied him in place. He gave the old road sign for 'roll 'em.' Beyond Columbia he showed up again.

His mouth moved like he was yelling me along, and his face twisted with as much fear as my own.

That gave me reason to hope. I'd never known Jesse to be afraid like that, so maybe there was a mistake. Maybe the dancing ghost wasn't the ghost of Jesse. I hung over the wheel and forced myself to think of Linda. When I thought of her I couldn't bring myself to get crazy. Highway 3 is not much of a road, but that's no bother. I can drive anything with wheels over any road ever made. The dancing ghost kept showing up and beckoning, telling me to scorch. I told myself the damn ghost had no judgment, or he wouldn't be a ghost in the first place.

That didn't keep me from pushing faster, but it wasn't fast enough to satisfy the roadside. They came out of the mist, or out of the ditches; crowds and clusters of ghosts standing pale beneath a weak moon. Some of them gossiped with each other. Some stood yelling me along. Maybe there was sense to it, but I had my hands full. If they were trying to help they sure weren't doing it. They just made me get my back up, and think of dropping revs.

Maybe the ghosts held a meeting and studied out the problem. They could see a clear road, but I couldn't. The dancing ghost showed up on highway 12 and gave me 'thumbs up' for a clear road. I didn't believe a word of it, and then I really didn't believe what showed in my mirrors. Headlights closed like I was standing. My feelings said that all of this had happened before; except last time there was only one set of headlights.

It was Miss Molly and Betty Lou that brought me home. Miss Molly overtook, sweeping past with a lane change smooth and sober as an Adventist. The high, slaunch-forward form of Miss Molly thrummed with business. She wasn't blowing sparks or showing off. She wasn't playing Gingerbread Man or tag.

Betty Lou came alongside so I could see who she was, then Betty Lou laid back a half mile. If we ran into a claim-jumping deputy, he'd have to chase her first; and more luck to him. Her headlights hovered back there like angels.

Miss Molly settled down a mile ahead of the Chrysler and stayed that distance, no matter how hard I pressed. Twice before Great Falls she spotted trouble, and her squinchy little brakelights hauled me down. Once it was an animal, and once it was busted road surface. Miss Molly and Betty Lou dropped me off before Great Falls, and picked me back up the minute I cleared town.

We ran the night like rockets. The roadside lay deserted. The dancing ghost stayed out of it, and so did the others. That let me concentrate, which proved a blessing. At those speeds a man don't have time to do deep thinking. The road rolls past, the hours roll, but you've got a racer's mind. No matter how tired you should be, you don't get tired until it's over.

I chased a ghost car northward while a fingernail moon moved across the sky. In deepest night the land turned silver. At speed you don't think, but you do have time to feel. The further north we pushed, the more my feelings went to despair. Maybe Miss Molly thought the same, but everybody did all they could.

The Chrysler was a howler, and Lord knows where the top end lay. I buried the needle. Even accounting for speedometer error, we burned along in the low half of the second century. We made highway 2 and Shelby around three in the morning, then hung a left. In just about no time I rolled home. Betty Lou dropped back and faded. Miss Molly blew sparks and purely flew out of sight. The sparks meant something. Maybe Miss Molly was still hopeful. Or, maybe she knew we were too late.

BENEATH THAT THIN MOON, MOUNDED GRAVES LOOKED LIKE dark surf across the acreage. No lights burned in the trailer, and the Linc showed nowhere. Even under the scant light you could see snowy tops of mountains, and the perfectly straight markers standing at the head of each grave. A tent, big enough to hold a small revival, stood not far from the trailer. In my headlights a sign on the tent read 'chapel.' I fetched a flashlight from the glove box.

A dozen folding chairs stood in the chapel, and a podium served as an altar. Jesse had rigged up two sets of candles, so I lit some. Matt Simons had written that the graveyard had to be seen to be believed. Hanging on one side of the tent was a sign reading 'shrine,' and all along that side hung roadmaps, and pictures of cars, and pictures of men standing beside their cars. There was a special display of odometers, with little cards beneath them: 330,938 miles, 407,000 miles, 'half a million miles more or less'. These were the championship cars, the all-time best at piling up road, and those odometers would make even a married man feel lonesome. You couldn't look at them without thinking of empty roads and empty nights.

Even with darkness spreading across the cemetery, nothing felt worse than the inside of that tent. I could believe that Jesse took it serious, and had tried to make it nice, but couldn't believe anyone else would buy it.

The night was not too late for owls, and nearly silent wings swept past as I left the tent. I walked to Miss Molly's grave, half expecting ghostly headlights. Two small markers stood beside a real fine marble headstone.

Potato
Happy-go-sloppy and good.
Rest In Peace Wherever You Are

Chip
A dandy little sidekicker
Running With Potato

From a distance I could see piled dirt where the dozer had dug new graves. I stepped cautious toward the dozer, not knowing why, but knowing it had to happen.

Two graves stood open like little garages, and the front ends of the Linc and the Hawk poked out. The Linc's front bumper shone spotless, but the rest of the Linc looked tough and experienced. Dents and dings crowded the sides, and cracked glass starred the windows.

The Hawk stood sparkly, ready to come roaring from the grave. Its glass shone washed and clean before my flashlight. I thought of what I heard in Sheridan, and thought of the first time I'd seen the Hawk. It hadn't changed. The Hawk looked like it had just been driven off a showroom floor.

Nobody in his right mind would want to look in those two cars, but it wasn't a matter of 'want.' Jesse, or Johnny—if that's who it was—had to be here someplace. It was certain-sure he needed help. When I looked, the Hawk sat empty. My flashlight poked against the glass of the Linc. Jesse lay there, taking his last nap across a car seat. His long black hair had turned to gray. He had always been thin, but now he was skin and bones. Too many miles, and no time to eat. Creases around his eyes came from looking at road, but now the creases were deep like an old man's. His eyes showed that he was dead. They were only open a little bit, but open enough.

I COULDN'T STAND TO BE ALONE WITH SUCH A SIGHT. IN LESS than fifteen minutes I stood banging on Matt Simon's door. Matt finally answered, and Nancy showed up behind him. She was in her robe. She stood taller than Matt, and sleepier. She looked blond and Swedish. Matt didn't know whether to be mad or glad. Then I got my story pieced together, and he really woke up.

"Dr. Jekyll has finally dealt with Mr. Hyde," he said in a low voice to Nancy. "Or, maybe the other way around." To me he said, "That may be a bad joke, but it's not ill meant." He went to get dressed. "Call Mike," he said to me. "Drunk or sober, I want him there."

Nancy showed me the phone. Then she went to the bedroom to talk with Matt. I could hear him soothing her fears. When Mike answered he was sleepy and sober, but he woke up stampeding.

Deep night and a thin moon is a perfect time for ghosts, but none showed up as Matt rode with me back to the graveyard. The Chrysler loafed. There was no need for hurry.

I told Matt what I'd learned in Sheridan.

"That matches what I heard," he said, "and we have two mysteries. The first mystery is interesting, but it's no longer important. Was John Still pretending to be Jesse Still, or was Jesse pretending to be John?"

"If Jesse drove into a river in '53, then it has to be John." I didn't like what I said, because Jesse was real. The best actor in the world couldn't pretend that well. My sorrow choked me, but I wasn't ashamed.

Matt seemed to be thinking along the same lines. "We don't know how long the game went on," he said real quiet.

202

"We never will know. John could have been playing at being Jesse way back in '53."

That got things tangled and I felt resentful. Things were complicated enough. Me and Matt had just lost a friend, and now Matt was talking like that was the least interesting part.

"Makes no difference whether he was John or Jesse," I told Matt. "He was Jesse when he died. He's laying across the seat in Jesse's car. Figure it anyway you want, but we're talking about Jesse."

"You're right," Matt said, "Also, you're wrong. We're talking about someone who was both." Matt sat quiet for a minute figuring things out. I told myself it was just as well that he'd married a schoolteacher. "Assume, for the sake of argument," he said, "that John was playing Jesse in '53. John drove into the river, and people believed they were burying Jesse.

"Or, for the sake of argument, assume that it was Jesse in '53. In that case the game started with John's grief. Either way, the game ran for many years." Matt was getting at something, but he always has to go roundabout.

"After years, John, or Jesse, disappeared. There was only a man who was both John and Jesse. That's the reason it makes no difference who died in '53."

Matt looked through the car window into the darkness like he expected to discover something important. "This is a long and lonesome country," he said. "The biggest mystery is: Why? The answer may lie in the mystery of twins, or it may be as simple as a man reaching into the past for happy memories. At any rate, one brother dies, and the survivor keeps his brother alive by living his brother's life, as well as his own. Think of the planning, the elaborate schemes, the near self-deception. Think of how often the roles shifted. A time must have arrived when that lonely man could not even remember who he was."

The answer was easy, and I saw it. Jesse, or John, chased the road to find something they'd lost on the road. They lost their parents and each other. I didn't say a damn word. Matt was making me mad, but I worked at forgiving him. He was handling his own grief, and maybe didn't have a better way.

"And so he invented the Road Dog," Matt said. "That kept the personalities separate. The Road Dog was a metaphor to make him proud. Perhaps it might confuse some of the ladies, but there isn't a man ever born who wouldn't understand it."

I remembered long nights and long roads. I couldn't fault his reasoning.

"At the same time," Matt said, "the metaphor served the twins. They could play road games with the innocence of children, maybe even replay memories of a time when their parents were alive and the world seemed warm. John played the Road Dog, and Jesse chased; and, by God, so did the rest of us. It was a magnificent metaphor."

"If it was that blamed snappy," I said, "how come it fell to pieces? For the last year it seems like Jesse's been running away from The Dog."

"The metaphor began to take over. The twins began to defend against each other," Matt said. "I've been watching it all along, but couldn't understand what was happening. John Still was trying to take over Jesse, and Jesse was trying to take over John."

"It worked for a long time," I said, "and then it didn't work. What's the kicker?"

"Our own belief," Matt said. "We all believed in the Road Dog. When all of us believed, John was forced to become stronger."

"And Jesse fought him off?"

"Successfully," Matt said. "All this year, when Jesse came firing out of town, rolling fifty miles, and firing back, I thought it was Jesse's problem. Now I see that John was trying to get free, get back on the road, and Jesse was dragging him back. This was a struggle between real men, maybe titans in the oldest sense, but certainly not imitations."

"It was a guy handling his problems."

"That's an easy answer. We can't know what went on with John," Matt said, "but we know some of what went on with Jesse. He tried to love a woman, Sarah, and failed. He lost his dogs which doesn't sound like much, unless your dogs are all you have. Jesse fought defeat by building his other metaphor which was that damned cemetery." Matt's voice got husky. He'd been holding in his sorrow, but his sorrow started coming through. It made me feel better about him.

"I think the cemetery was Jesse's way of answering John, or denying that he was vulnerable. He needed a symbol. He tried to protect his loves and couldn't. He couldn't even protect his love for his brother. That cemetery is the last bastion of Jesse's love." Matt looked like he was going to cry, and I felt the same.

"Cars can't hurt you," Matt said. "Only bad driving hurts you. The cemetery is a symbol for protecting one of the few loves you can protect. That's not saying anything bad about Jesse. That's saying something with sadness for all of us."

I slowed to pull onto Jesse's place. Mike's Olds sat by the trailer. Lights were on in the trailer, but no other lights showed anywhere.

"Men build all kinds of worlds in order to defeat fear and loneliness," Matt said. "We give and take as we build those worlds. One must wonder how much Jesse, and John, gave in order to take the little that they got."

We climbed from the Chrysler as autumn wind moved across the graveyard and felt its way toward my bones. The moon lighted faces of grave markers, but not enough that you could read them.

Mike had the bulldozer warming up. It stood and puttered, and darkness felt best and Mike knew it. The headlights were off. Far away on highway 2 an engine wound tight and squalling, and it seemed like echoes of engines whispered among the graves. Mike stood huge as a grizzly.

"I've shot horses that looked healthier than you two guys," he said, but said it sort of husky.

Matt motioned toward the bulldozer. "This is illegal."

"Nobody ever claimed it wasn't." Mike was ready to fight if a fight was needed. "Anybody who don't like it can turn around and walk."

"I like it," Matt said. "It's fitting and proper. But, if we're caught there's hell to pay."

"I like most everything and everybody," Mike said, "except the government. They paw a man to death while he's alive, then keep pawing his corpse. I'm saving Jesse a little trouble."

"They like to know that he's dead and what killed him."

"Sorrow killed him," Mike said. "Let it go at that."

Jesse killed himself, timing his tiredness and starvation just right, but I was willing to let it go, and Matt was too.

"We'll go along with you," Matt said. "But, they'll sell this place for taxes. Somebody will start digging sometime."

"Not for years and years. It's deeded to me. Jesse fixed up papers. They're on the kitchen table." Mike turned toward the trailer. "We're going to do this right, and there's not much time."

We found a blanket and a quilt in the trailer. Mike opened a kitchen drawer and pulled out snapshots. Some looked pretty new, and some were faded: a man and woman in old fashioned clothes, a picture of two young boys in Sunday suits, pictures of cars and roadsigns, and pictures of two women who were maybe Sue Ellen and Sarah. Mike piled them like a deck of cards, snapped a rubber band around them, and checked the trailer. He picked up a pair of pale yellow sunglasses that some racers use for night driving. "You guys see anything else?"

"His dogs," Matt said. "He had pictures of his dogs."

We found them under a pillow, and it didn't pay to think why they were there. Then we went to the Linc and wrapped Jesse real careful in the blanket. We spread the quilt over him, and laid his stuff on the floor beside the accelerator. Then Mike remembered something. He half unwrapped Jesse, went through his pockets, then wrapped him back up. He took Jesse's keys and left them hanging in the ignition.

The three of us stood beside the Linc, and Matt cleared his throat.

"It's my place to say it," Mike told him. "This was my best friend." Mike took off his cap. Moonlight lay thin on his bald head:

"A lot of preachers will be glad this man is gone, and that's one good thing you can say for him. He drove nice people crazy. This man was a hellion pure and simple; but what folks don't understand is hellions have their place. They put everything on the line over nothing very much. Most guys worry so much about dying they never do any living. Jesse was so alive with living he never gave dying any thought. This man would roll 90 just to get to a bar before it closed." Mike kind of choked up and stopped to listen. From the graveyard came the echoes of engines, and from highway 2 rose the thrum of a straight-eight crankshaft whipping in its bed. Dim light covered the graveyard, like a hundred sets of parking lights and not the moon.

"This man kept adventure alive, when every place else it's dying. There was nothing ever smug or safe about this man. If he had fears he laughed. This man never hit a woman or crossed a friend. He did tie the can on Betty Lou one night, but can't be blamed. It was really The Dog who did that one. Jesse never had a problem until he climbed into that Studebaker."

So Mike had known all along. At least Mike knew something.

"I could always run even with Jesse," Mike said, "but I never could beat The Dog. The Dog could clear any track. And in a damn Studebaker."

"But a very swift Studebaker," Matt muttered, like a Holy Roller answering the preacher.

"Bored and stroked and rowdy," Mike said, "and you can say the same for Jesse. Let that be the final word. Amen."

IV

A little spark of flame dwelt at the stack of the dozer, and
distant mountains lay white-capped and prophesied
winter. Mike filled the graves quick. Matt got rakes and a
shovel. I helped him mound the graves with only moonlight
to go on, while Mike went to the trailer. He made coffee.

"Drink up and git," Mike told us when he poured the
coffee.

"Jesse's got some friends who need to visit, and it will be
morning pretty quick."

"Let them," Matt said. "We're no hindrance."

"You're a smart man," Mike told Matt, "but your
smartness makes you dumb. You started to hinder the night
you stopped driving beyond your headlights." Mike didn't
know how to say it kind, so he said it rough. His red mustache
and bald head made him look like a pirate in a picture.

"You're saying that I'm getting old." Matt has known
Mike long enough not to take offense.

"Me too," Mike said, "but not that old. When you get old you stop seeing them. Then you want to stop seeing them. Then you want to stop seeing them. You get afraid for your hide."

"You stop imagining?"

"Shitfire," Mike said, "you stop seeing. Imagination is something you use when you don't have eyes." He pulled a cigar out of his shirt pocket and was chawing it before he ever got it lit. "Ghosts have lost it all. Maybe they're the ones the Lord didn't love well enough. If you see them, but ain't one, maybe you're important."

Matt mulled that, and so did I. We've both wailed a lot of road for some sort of reason.

"They're kind of rough," Matt said about ghosts. "They hitch rides but don't want 'em. I've stopped for them and got laughed at. They fool themselves, or maybe they don't."

"It's a young man's game," Matt said.

"It's a game guys got to play. Jesse played the whole deck. He was who he was, whenever he was it. That's the key. That's the reason you slug cops when you gotta. It looks like Jesse died old, but he lived young longer than most. That's the real mystery. How does a fella keep going?"

"Before we leave," I said, "how long did you know that Jesse was The Dog?"

"Maybe a year and a half. About the time he started running crazy."

"And never said a word?"

Mike looked at me like something you'd wipe off your boot.

"Learn to ride your own fence," he told me. "It was Jesse's business." Then he felt sorry for being rough. "Besides," he said, "we were having fun. I expect that's all over now."

Matt followed me to the Chrysler. We left the cemetery feeling tired and mournful. I shoved the car onto highway 2, heading toward Matt's place.

"Wring it out once for old times?"

"Putter along," Matt said. "I just entered the putter-stage of life, and may as well practice doing it."

In my mirrors a stream of headlights showed, then vanished one by one as cars turned into the graveyard. The moon had left the sky. Over toward South Dakota was a suggestion of first faint morning light. Mounded graves lay at my elbow, and so did Canada. On my left the road south ran fine and fast as a man can go. Mist rose from the roadside ditches, and maybe there was movement in the mist, maybe not.

THERE'S LITTLE MORE TO TELL. THROUGH FALL AND WINTER and spring and summer I drove to Sheridan. The Mormon turned out to be a pretty good man, for a Mormon. I kept at it, and drove through another autumn and another winter. Linda got convinced. We got married in the spring, and I expected trouble. Married people are supposed to fight, but nothing like that ever happened. We just worked hard, got our own place in a few years, and Linda birthed two girls. That disappointed the Mormon, but was a relief to me.

And in those seasons of driving, when the roads were good for twenty mile an hour in snow, or eighty under sun, the road stood empty except for a couple times. Miss Molly showed up once early on to say a bridge was out. She might have showed up another time. Squinchy little taillights winked one night when it was late and I was highballing. Some guy jack-knifed a Freightliner, and his trailer lay across the road.

But I saw no other ghosts. I'd like to say that I saw the twins, John and Jesse standing by the road, giving the high sign or dancing, but it never happened.

I did think of Jesse, though, and thought of one more thing. If Matt was right, then I saw how Jesse had to die before I got home. He had to, because I believed in Road Dog. My belief would have been just enough to bring John forward, and that would have been fatal too. If either one of them became too strong, they both of them lost. So Jesse had to do it.

The graveyard sank beneath the weather. Mike tended it for awhile, but lost interest. Weather swept the mounds flat. Weed-covered markers tumbled to decay and dust, so that only one marble headstone stands solid beside highway 2. The marker doesn't bend before the winter winds, nor does the little stone that me and Mike and Matt put there. It lays flat against the ground. You have to know where to look:

Road Dog
1931–1965
2 million miles more-or-less
Run and run as fast as we can
We never can catch the Gingerbread Man

And now, even the great good cars are dead, or most of them. What with gas prices and wars and rumors of wars the cars these days are all suspensions. They'll corner like a cat, but don't have the scratch of a cat; and maybe that's a good thing. The state posts fewer crosses.

Still, there are some howlers left out there, and some guys are still howling. I lie in bed of nights and listen to the scorch of engines along highway 2. I hear them claw the darkness, stretching lonesome at the sky, scatting across the eternal land; younger guys running as young guys must; chasing each other, or chasing the land of dreams, or chasing into ghostland while hoping it ain't true—guys running into darkness chasing each other, or chasing something—chasing road.

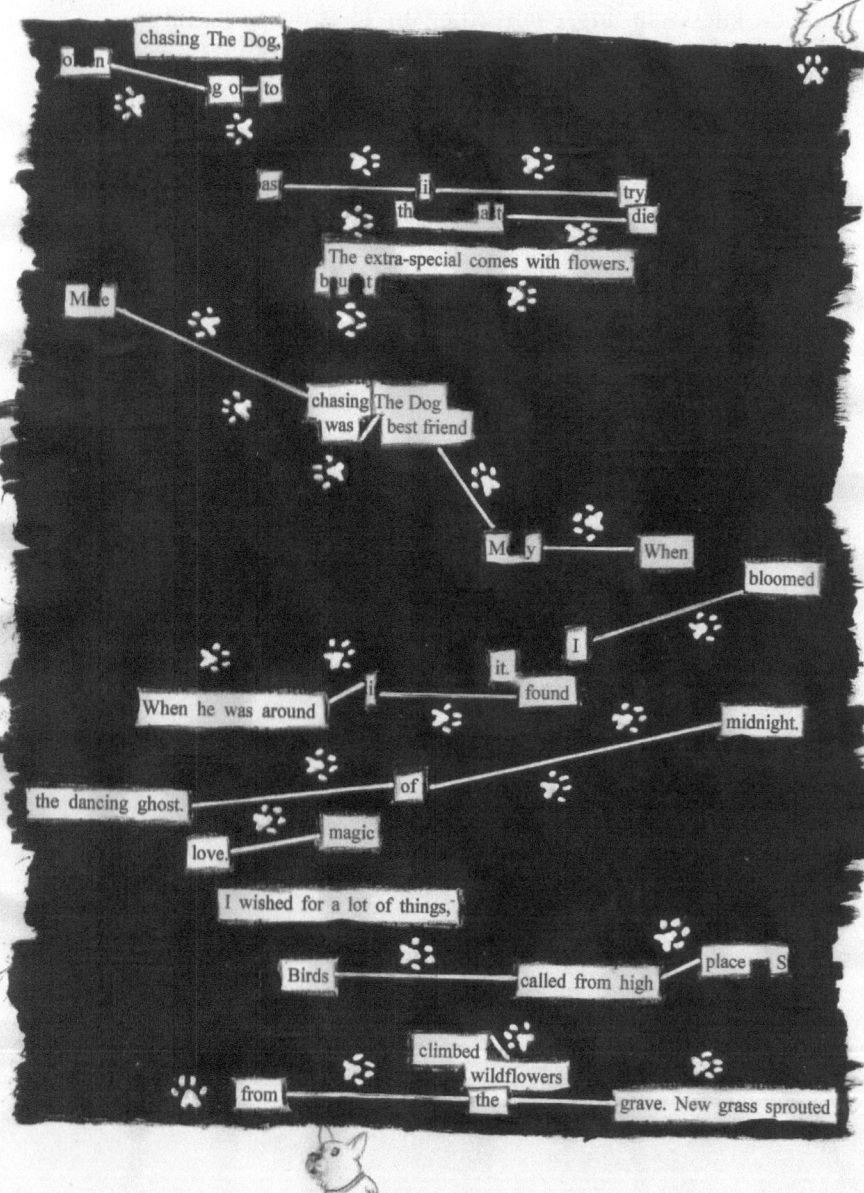

chasing The Dog,

often

go to

as i try

th at die

The extra-special comes with flowers.
bought

Mike

chasing The Dog
was best friend

Molly When

bloomed

I

it.
found

When he was around i

midnight.

the dancing ghost. of

love. magic

I wished for a lot of things,

Birds called from high place S

climbed
wildflowers
from the grave. New grass sprouted

ABOUT THE AUTHORS

HARLAN ELLISON OFTEN SAID, "IT'S EASY TO BECOME A WRITER but hard to stay a writer." **Mort Castle** agrees. His first novel came out in 1967 and, in 2024, 40th anniversary editions of his horror classic The Strangers, lauded in Grady Hendrix's Paperbacks from Hell, will be published in Spain, Poland and Germany, and in the USA by Cemetery Dance. Castle's won three Bram Stoker Awards® and two Black Quills, and has been nominated for the Shirley Jackson award, the International Horror Guild Award, the Pushcart Prize, the Audie, and others. He and Jane, his wife of 52 years, reside in Crete, Illinois, where they sometimes sit on the front porch, watching sunsets while Castle plays banjo.

D. T. FRIEDMAN LIVES IN NEW YORK WITH A FORMER STREET cat named Kimble.

GWENDOLYN KISTE IS THE THREE-TIME BRAM STOKER AWARD-winning author of *The Rust Maidens, Reluctant Immortals, Boneset & Feathers, Pretty Marys All in a Row*, and *The Haunting of Velkwood*. Her short fiction and nonfiction have appeared in outlets including Lit Hub, Nightmare, Best American Science Fiction and Fantasy, Vastarien, Tor Nightfire, Titan Books, and The Dark. She's a Lambda Literary Award winner, and her fiction has also received the This Is Horror award for Novel of the Year as well as nominations for the Premios Kelvin, Ignotus, and Dragon Awards. Originally from Ohio, she now resides on an abandoned horse farm outside of Pittsburgh with her husband, their excitable calico cat, and not nearly enough ghosts. Find her online at gwendolynkiste.com

JACK CADY WON THE ATLANTIC MONTHLY "FIRST" AWARD IN 1965 for his story, "The Burning." He continued writing and authored nearly a dozen novels, one book of critical analysis of American literature, and more than fifty short stories. Over the course of his literary career, he won the Iowa Prize for Short Fiction, the National Literary Anthology Award, the Washington State Governor's Award, the Nebula Award, the Bram Stoker Award, and the World Fantasy Award. Prior to a lengthy career in education, Jack worked as a tree high climber, a Coast Guard seaman, an auctioneer, and a long-distance truck driver. He held teaching positions at the University of Washington, Clarion College, Knox College, the University of Alaska at Sitka, and Pacific Lutheran University. He spent many years living in Port Townsend, Washington and died in 2004.

HENRY FERRIS ARNOLD IS ANOTHER "LOST" AUTHOR FROM the days of the pulps, something that is quite surprising since "The Night Wire" was considered the most popular story ever published in Weird Tales. What few sources give any information about his life say that he was born in 1901, worked as an author and journalist and died in 1963, but even these sketchy details (and his actual name, for that matter) may, or may, not, be true. All that is known as fact about Arnold, is that his fictional output, at least in the fields of science fiction and horror, consisted of only 3 works: "The Night Wire", appearing in Weird Tales in 1926; "The City of Iron Cubes," serialized in the March and April issues of Weird Tales and a two-part serial "When Atlantis Was," that appeared in the October and December 1937 issues of Amazing Stories. Outside of that, Arnold remains an enigma.

ABOUT THE EDITOR

Kevin Lucia is the eBook and trade paperback editor at Cemetery Dance Publications. His short fiction has been published in many venues, most notably with Neil Gaiman, Clive Barker, David Morell, Peter Straub, Bentley Little, and Robert McCammon. His first novel, The Horror at Pleasant Brook, was published by Crystal Lake Publishing, October 2023.

Cemetery Dance Publications Paperbacks and Ebooks!

THE PLASTIC PRIEST
by Nicole Cushing

When the soul has been thoroughly poisoned, the body must abandon it. Everything feels unreal afterwards, but plastic heads shed no tears. Bram Stoker Award® winning author Nicole Cushing offers an excursion into the Weird, a quiet novella of a madwoman in a mad town, as an Episcopal priest grapples with the meaning of faith, reality, and if there is anything real to either of them, at the end of it all.

"Nicole Cushing is one of the sharpest, most innovative writers in the field today."
—Thomas Tessier

GOD MACHINE,
Greg F. Gifune

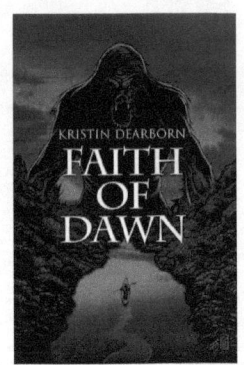

In a hotel room on Cape Cod, a troubled young prostitute brutally takes her own life, leaving cryptic clues as to why written in blood on the walls. When head of hotel security and former cop Chris Tallo finds her savaged body, he sets out to discover why the woman committed suicide in such a vicious manner.

"The best writer of horror novels and supernatural thrillers at work today."
—Christopher Rice

FAITH OF DAWN,
by Kristen Dearborn

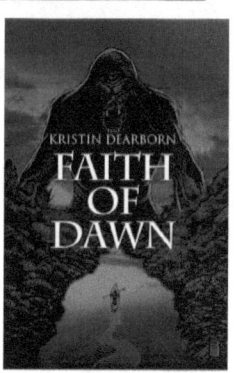

Private Investigator Amanda Lane thought she'd gotten her life together after losing her leg in Afghanistan, but a crumbling marriage and PTSD showed her that couldn't be farther from the truth.

"Kristin Dearborn is one of the most talented under-the-radar writers the horror genre has to offer."
—Christopher Golden, *New York Times* bestselling author of *Road of Bones* and *All Hallows*

Purchase these and other fine works of horror from Cemetery Dance Publications today!
https://www.cemeterydance.com/

HORROR DNA
MOVIES
COMIC BOOKS
MUSIC
BOOKS
VIDEO GAMES
IT'S IN OUR BLOOD
horrordna.com